Hell For The Company

DICK DENNY

Foundations, LLC.
Brandon, MS 39047
www.foundationsbooks.net

Hell for the Company
By: Dick Denny

Cover by: Dawné Dominique
Edited by: Steve Soderquist
Author photo by: Sharon Hamilton

Published in the United States of America
Worldwide Electronic & Digital Rights
Worldwide English Language Print Rights

ISBN-13: 978-1985190702
ISBN-10: 1985190702

Acknowledgements

I want to thank the whole Foundations team for putting up with my crazy.
There is plenty of crazy to put up with...

Table of Contents

"Everyone knows God protects Drunkards and Lovers."

- Alexandre Dumas

Prologue: The End of the Beginning

The world lit up as the lightening cracked across the sky. Water dripped down the walls and pooled onto the alley. My suit was soaked and water streamed down my face; my usually unruly hair matted to my head. I looked down the alley and saw him standing there in his long, gracefully flowing violet trench coat and cowboy hat.

"It's easy, Nick... all you have to do is give me the Sword." His voice was a thick molasses. It sounded like the bastard child of Barry White and a Glacier.

I raised my 1911 and aimed the .45 ACP pistol, gripped in the modern isosceles stance. Proper grip, proper sight picture, I thumbed the hammer back.

"You know that's not going to work on me. At worst it's a bee sting, at best it's a nuisance." His voice rumbled through the downpour.

I knew he was right. I let the pistol slide from my right hand to my left and fall to my side. I looked down at my right hand. I thought about Uncle Lew. I thought about Gretchen and wondered if she was even alive. I thought about my trashed car. I thought about my smashed bottle of Macallan 18. I thought about my wrecked office door. I thought about my dead goddamned mom. I felt angry. I felt mad. I felt pissed the fuck off.

I watched the pommel materialize in my palm and my fingers curled around it. I heard the hiss of water turning to steam as it landed on the growing blade. A blade made of fire.

"Good." He smiled. "Give me The Sword, Nick, and all this ends. You can have your life back."

I looked at the Fiery Sword, and then I looked to the Archangel at the end of the alley dressed like a very expensive 70's pimp. "You want the Fiery Sword, Zadkiel?" I gestured with the .45 in my left hand. "Then *Molan Labe*, you piece of shit."

Zadkiel smiled. "You know that is plural in the Ancient Greek."

I sighed. "Goddammit..."

"Watch the blasphemy please." There was a crack in the glacier voice as if an iceberg was breaking off.

"Fuck you." I slowly shook my head and lifted the Fiery Sword. "You want it you piece of shit, come get take it from me Charlton Heston style."

Zadkiel took off his cowboy hat and ran his hand over his smooth hairless head that was somehow still glowing even soaked in the storm. "I'm not familiar with Heston style."

I was about to get my ass kicked, probably killed, horribly. "Out of my cold dead hand, motherfucker."

If heaven is a place where the angels go,
Well then I've got a story to tell.
If heaven is a place where the angels go,
Then I know I'm going straight to Hell!

"Little Smirk" Theory of a Deadman

I. Hot as a Bill Murray Movie

So, the day you put your Mom in the dirt is supposed to suck, but that doesn't quite cover the weirdness of my day. Dad had died a few years before. He'd literally walked through a door at work and fell over dead; His heart just gave out. Which in retrospect is probably the way to go; here one second, gone the next. Looks out for the bus... what bus? Splat.

Mom was stabbed to death. I got to the hospital after it was done, disheveled, and if I'm honest, hung over. The doctor pulled the sheet down to show me her face. All the paperwork had been taken care of before I got there. Good old Uncle Lew, mom's big brother. He was the only person in Mom's family I'd ever met and also literally the coolest person I'd ever met. Dad's dislike of the man had done nothing but endear me to him.

Too bad Uncle Lew wasn't around.

Now I stood in the rain as the preacher droned on about Gods love and redemption and heavenly reward and blah blah blah. I looked across the grave and saw my brother crying like a baby; that was to be expected. His wife looked bored. His ex-wife looked genuinely saddened but to be honest, I couldn't care less. His brood of six kids all looked bored and uncomfortable. Two from his first marriage, two from his second, and his second wife's two daughters from her first marriage.

I loved those kids in the obligatory way but not because any of us had earned it. The cost of the wars between me and my family was the hope of any kinship with my nieces and nephews. In spiting my brother and parents, I shot the shit out of any chance of a relationship I might have had with the next generation. That was the only thing I regretted. Then again, that's normal. I never put in any effort with my Aunts and Uncles either. I get it's mostly my fault, but still. They knew my phone number and email. I'm not hard to find. My failure was in failing to maintain a relationship with them, their failure was in their natural lack of effort to have one with me. Still, it was ever going to be judged on my head. Who blames kids for that kind of thing? I don't. I know it's my fault.

I could put my hands in my pockets and wouldn't be able to find a fuck to give about any adult on the other side of the grave.

The preacher finished, and my brother came over and wrapped his arms around me whether I cared for it or not.

"Nick..." he sobbed in my shoulder already wet with rain.

"Yeah." I gently pushed him back when he didn't let go and stuffed my hands in the pocket of my suit. Black slacks, black jacket, rumpled white shirt, and beat up black and white Chuck Taylor's all damp in the misting rain. My unruly hair matted to my head. My pistol sat under my left arm with two spare magazines under my right. "Thanks. Do I need to sign anything?"

I didn't mean to sound cold, but I didn't see a reason to get emotional. I'd rather deal with the lawyer shit sooner than later. I'd broken with my parents' a while ago. I didn't want a damned thing and the quicker we were done with paperwork, the quicker I could ignore my brother with the equal vigor that I had been for the past four years. My family and I had come to the impasse between them not approving of the life I chose to lead, and me not giving a shit.

I'd been following a married woman all night and finally got the pictures I needed of her strapping on a strap on and giving her boss a probing to justify the two weeks' worth charging the daily rate and expenses it was costing the cuck'ed husband. I hadn't had a drink in four hours and my flask weighed heavy in my pocket.

I took it out and started unscrewing the top but stopped when I heard him sob. "No, I'm sorry..."

"Cool." I took a slug from the flask then slid it back in my jacket before I stuffed my hands in my pants pockets and started walking off. If you don't know what's going to happen, and you're buzzed, it's better to maintain the buzz than it is to be caught off guard while coming down from it. I walked out of the cemetery and made my way to where I left my car on the street. I found another ticket on the windshield of my mid 90's Miata, soon to find a home with the growing collection of tickets in the glove compartment. More importantly, I found the duct tape holding the soft top together was starting to fray. I threw the ticket way and added more duct tape. It looked like it was going to be a stormy day and I didn't need my shitty leather car seats getting shittier.

It was ten thirty in the morning and I was hungry. I got in the car and cranked the heat to try and dry off before putting the car in gear. I knew they'd already be serving lunch. I drove from the cemetery to Sharky's, which was not the greatest of strip clubs. In fact, it was like a museum for track marks, C-Section scars, stretch marks, irregular moles that doctors should look at, and strippers too past their prime to work at Titanium Lightening. But what Sharky's did have, was a killer kitchen. I don't tend to like buffets, but damn Sharky's was good.

Fat Craig was working the door, which was better than Mole-Face McDouchbag who hated me because I beat the spread for the last Super Bowl. I gave Fat Craig five bucks even though he made no motion to charge me the cover.

The lights were dim, thank God. It was the sick combination of dark neon and strobe with mind numbing techno music pumping through dilapidated speakers. But God the chicken fingers were that perfect combination of moist and crispy, the curly fries were decadent enough to have taken part in a Roman orgy and the mini-steaks were a perfect non-fatty medium with a lovely Au Jus. It was dark enough that the plate looked clean too.

"What are you drinking, Nick?" C-Section Sapphire asked me. She was wearing a leather bikini top and daisy dukes. She could have worn more for my tastes, but you get what you pay for.

"The usual." I sat at a booth doing the best I could to not look at the Tuesday pre-lunch stripper crew. It was slightly depressing that I was here enough to have a usual, but I didn't let it bring me down.

C-Section Sapphire brought me a tumbler with more than the normal amount of eighteen-year-old Macallan that lived behind the bar and was only served to me, because I put it there.

Sharky's was not a movie strip club. It wasn't gorgeous women scantily clad in decent low light. Bushes were bared with enough abundance to be capable of becoming topiary with the proper management. Tits were on display in varying degrees of asymmetry. The floor was movie theater sticky. The neon flickered, the sound system cracked and popped. The whole place felt like a Hepatitis petri dish.

I sat and actively avoided looking at anything other than my plate. And then I heard the song. I'd like to say it was reflex, but it was more curiosity that drew my eyes to the stage.

If stripping were an Olympic Event, Def Leppard's *Pour Some Sugar on Me* would become the national anthem. I wondered who would have the audacity to try and dance to that most sacred of stripper hymns. I had the notion that it would be one of the usual Sharky's Girls, however I was wrong — so wrong that I didn't mind at all.

She was the perfect American. Her family tree had to have Asian and European and Native-American, or others, not enough of anything to be one thing. Her hair was as black as sin filled dreams that excited you but are so weird you'd never admit that it turned you on, and frankly, you don't understand why it got you going to start with. Her eyes were dark but shined like crime stains under an investigators black light. She was short, barely 5'1" or 5'2". Her body was as tight as the script of the movie *Groundhog Day*. I saw she had two sets of tattoos; the first, a gothic cross tramp stamp. It felt German but without a Nazi connotation to detract from the allure. The second was a pair of red and gold angel style wings starting at her shoulder blades, raising up to her shoulders then down her upper arms, over her elbows and down her forearms ending at her wrists. She moved like a trained dancer and her clothes came off with a tantalizingly seductive pace. She'd started off dressed like a cop, but that illusion was already as dead as my hopes for Social Security, but there was a joy to the way she moved. She was not a normal Sharky's Tuesday morning girl. That's why I made the greatest mistake a man can make in a strip club... eye contact. Her eyes met mine and to my surprise, she smiled.

After that it was like her dance was only for me. But to be fair I was the only patron that time of day that could be defined as "A Drunk" as opposed to "A Junkie." I watched her dance, which was half dance and half professional gymnast floor routine. I knew watching her that if I were the Key Master and she was the Gate Keeper and us doing it would unleash Gozer the Destructor upon the world... I would be ok with those consequences. Who wouldn't?

The song finished and from off-stage someone tossed her a pair of black lacy boy-cut panties. She tugged them on while collecting the cash on the stage. She smiled as she tucked the cash in the black garter on her left thigh. She took another bow, then instead of going back stage she ran, hand planted, and flipped in the air before really sticking the landing off-stage.

The next thing I knew, before the Junkies could get to her, she moved and slid into the booth across from me. She reached over and grabbed one of my chicken fingers and bit into it with delicious languidity.

"Yes," I said.

She smiled as she chewed, which I didn't think was possible. I watched her swallow and received the heartening news she had no Adam's apple.

"Yes what?" There was sultriness to her voice that gave no hint of the emphysema or other respiratory disease that normally accompanied a Sharky's girl. I was convinced at least one of them had tuberculosis.

"You may have one of my chicken fingers." I took another bite myself.

"Well, that's interesting." She arched her eyebrow. "Very interesting."

"What is?" She had caught me a bit off guard, besides being topless and gorgeous and talking to me, neither of which seemed plausible in the setting.

"Can is a question of ability." She bit into the chicken finger and didn't speak till she finished chewing. "May is a question of permission. Most people don't know the difference or even if they do they mess it up, so..." she leaned her head in. "Interesting."

I was doing a really good job of not looking at her bare perky tits. Good, but not perfect.

I sipped my scotch but as I sat my glass down she took the glass. I smirked. "Help yourself."

She sipped the scotch then waved for the waitress ordering two more. "So, most overrated band of the 90's?" Her fingers brushed mine as she handed back to me my half empty tumbler.

"What?" She was lobbing random balls over the plate and I was definitely missing them. Usually conversations had a predictable pattern. She was either ignorant of, or simply disregarding the standard forms of communication.

She smiled and gestured to her tits like a presenter on The Price is Right. "I figured we were past the normal getting to know you conversation." She paused. "And now you're staring."

"Well that's not my fault, is it?" I managed to look up. "The Bare-Naked Ladies."

She smiled. "Well that's ironic, isn't it?" I chuckled then she asked. "Best song of the 90's?"

"Well, it's not Alanis Morrissette's *Ironic*. It's gotta be *Closing Time* by Semisonic." I answered that one a little too fast. "Why are you asking about the nineties?"

She shrugged. "I was six when the nineties ended, so I'm curious."

That made me feel old. Well, there goes the five-year rule.

"So what's your name?" she asked with a smile.

"Honestly?" I finished off the tumbler of scotch and set the empty glass to the side.

She nodded coyly.

"Woodrow Wilson Smith, I hate my freaking parents for naming me that." I bit into a chicken finger. "I mean, why couldn't they have just named me John."

"That's Lazarus Long." She bit her lip seductively as she said it. Her eyes gleamed as she'd caught me in the lie.

I sighed. "You're right, that's a Heinlein character."

"He's a great writer." She smiled and leaned back, lacing her fingers behind her head.

"I'm Dwayne Hicks." I tossed a curly fry in my mouth and kept my eyes locked to hers.

She raised an eyebrow. "That's Michael Biehn in *Aliens*."

"God he's a great actor." I shook my head.

"He's the world's best Navy Seal." She nodded.

"God yes, I'm betting he's the dude who actually shot Bin Laden." I couldn't help but chuckle.

She put her hands on the table and cocked her head to the side. "That theory holds up to scrutiny."

"I'm Jim Gavin." Jim Gavin was usually the name I told girls in bars. That way they couldn't track me down.

She laughed at that one. "You look good for the WWII commander of the 82nd Airborne."

"Okay, seriously, I'm Nick Adams." Well, it was half true anyway.

She smiled and raised an eyebrow. "So, what was Hemingway like? Or should I ask Robert Jordan or Fredrick Henry or an old man to go fishing with?"

Christ she was good. "Sturm Brightblade?"

"Would that make me Kitiara uth Matar?" She laughed. She then leaned forward even more excited. "Would our son be Steel?"

"I dunno, have you ever made out with a half-elf or have a near giant or scrawny half-brothers?" I cocked my eyebrow.

"Isn't Dragon Lance great?" Her smile was sweet enough to make a man diabetic.

"Yeah, it is." There were better fantasy series, but I've never regretted the time I've given Dragon Lance. "Okay, honestly. I'm Will Munny."

She'd dropped her voice low doing her best impression of Clint Eastwood, which wasn't very good. "You've killed women and kids, and everything that's walked and crawled, and now you're here to kill Little Bill for what he did to Ned?"

Okay, now she was just playing with me. It would be cruel, but she was mostly naked, so I wasn't going to throw a flag on the play.

"So,- why are you talking to me?" I rested my elbows on the table, leaning in. Better to change the subject than to let her win outright.

"What do you mean?" She leaned back and crossed her arms under her breasts, which didn't help anything under my end of the table. I felt her ankle start rubbing my calf through my slacks.

"Nothing about this is right?" I finished my scotch as C-Section Sapphire brought the second.

"Please explain." Her smile was inquisitive.

"You're gorgeous, and not like stripper gorgeous, but legitimately gorgeous. You don't belong here. You actually have dancing talent. You don't have C-Section scars or stretch marks. You don't have track marks. You're confident. You shouldn't be here." I gestured around the second-rate strip club with a first-rate buffet. "And why the hell are you talking to me?"

"You want the truth?" She bit her lower lip seductively.

I shrugged and became aware of the feel of my 1911 under my arm. For the first time, I felt like I might need the pistol I habitually carried.

She smiled and leaned in. "Your name is Nick Decker, your mom died earlier this week and I'm here to protect you."

I looked at her tits again... I couldn't help it. "Wait, how the fuck do you know my name?" I could have sounded calmer, cooler asking, but it came out too fast.

She smiled. "I'm a member of *Qui Ordinis Fratrum et Sororum Germanica Domus Sanctae Mariae in Jerusalem, et in umbra*."

"The fuck?" I knew my jaw dropped. I was never going to win the World Series of Poker with her at the table, not topless anyway. "The fuck does that fuckin' mean?"

"The Order of Brothers of the German House of Saint Mary in Jerusalem Sisters in Shadow." There was no irony or humor to her voice. She seemed completely serious in the crazy she was talking.

They say, *never stick your dick in crazy,* so this was freaking torture.

"Okay, crazy, I'm willing to let you sit without a top and keep talking. Protect me from what?"

"My name is Gretchen and I'm here to protect you, there are organizations that want to bring you down and take what you have." She reached across the booth to grab my hand. Her hands were soft, and they felt nice.

"And what pray tell would I have?" I asked sarcastically.

She answered with total sincerity and a complete lack of postmodern irony or self-awareness. "A great and powerful holy relic."

I would have laughed, but her tits were still out.

II. The Weirdest Things Can Sustain an Erection

You don't stick your dick in crazy. It is a general rule that is well worth following.

I'd like to say I didn't know why I was out front of Sharky's waiting for an obviously insane stripper, but I did. She was hot. Plain and simple. I'd like to say I had a better reason, but my head was wrapped around her tits and tight ass. Planning ahead has never been my strong suit and gals that hot just don't have anything to do with guys like me. So crazy or not, I waited for her.

If she was hot with her clothes off, then believe it or not she was hotter clothed, not that there was a lot to be left to the imagination. She wore a top that was more a gray sports bra than any other type of top I could describe with the red lettering that read, "All I Want Is Sandwiches And Hot Dirty Sex." Her black jacket had full sleeves but the torso and back was cut above her midriff. She had a two-diamond belly button ring. Her short black short shorts, which might as well have been panties, were circled with a belt that had an assortment of pouches and silver chains. She had on thigh high fishnet stockings and a highly polished pair of Army issue jungle boots. If she had been shopping at *Hot-Sluts-R-Us*, she definitely pulled from the "Objectify-Me" collection.

If this were a movie, Guns N' Roses *Paradise City* would be playing as she danced out the door seductively in that outfit, and I would replay that scene over and over, at various speeds.

She looked so hot I didn't notice the gym bag she was carrying.

"What?" she asked with a coy smile as she pushed her hip out playfully.

"I'm just getting a good mental picture to fill the spank bank for later."

She laughed. "You were paying attention earlier, right?"

I shrugged. "What? Fantasy is about storyline as much as it is about mental visual stimuli." Why the hell was I telling her that? That was guy secret 101.

She walked over and wrapped her arm through mine. "Where's your car?"

We started walking and I felt her leaning to my side. I gestured down the road toward the Miata by the unpaid meter.

She smiled and rubbed up under my arm. "That a 1911?"

"Good guess." A lot of girls would freak out and say, "A gun? Really?" But she'd figured out the type just from the feel through the jacket. That was impressive.

She shrugged. "It was in the report."

"So if you got reports on me, tell me something about you."

She started listing and the way she put it, it sounded matter of fact, not like she was bragging. "Well, I have black belts in Aikido and Jeet Kune Do…" Her tone implied it wasn't especially special, because didn't everyone have black belts in Aikido and Jeet Kune Do?

"Of course you do," I said with a sigh.

"I prefer the 9mm where you obviously like .45 ACP's… when it comes to automatics anyway." She smiled sweetly. Implying she didn't care for semiautomatic pistols.

"Well, yeah, cause I'm a man." 9mm was for women and government types.

She bit her lip playfully. "A real man, eh? I'm a polyglot but only of fictional languages."

I looked down to her confused. "What?"

She laughed. "Polyglot means I speak multiple languages."

"I know that!" I laughed so it didn't sound like I was offended she didn't think I knew what polyglot meant. "What languages?"

She raised her eyebrows and shrugged. "I speak Vulcan, Klingon, Sindarin and Dothraki."

"Nerd."

She laughed. "I'm a nerd because you're a dork."

"I mean Star Trek?"

"Well, we didn't find out you hated Star Trek until after I'd learned Vulcan and Klingon."

"Yeah, you and your secret society?" My voice dripped with sarcasm.

"That's right." She leaned her head on my upper arm. "Your turn."

"For what?" I shot her a sideways glance as we turned the corner.

"Why did you become a P.I?"

"Money." I said it flatly, blunt, and true.

"But what do you get out of it?"

"Money." I didn't know what she was digging for there.

"But how does it make you feel? Rewarded, satisfied?"

"Less poor?" I couldn't tell if that was a declarative statement or a question, because even when I get paid I was still pretty freaking poor.

"What would you rather be doing than being a P.I?"

"You." I didn't think about that, I just said it. I waited for a slap that didn't come. I look down and saw her smile bigger than someone a near stranger had just admitted non-PG desires should.

We stopped at the car and she moved to face me. "Are you going to open the door for me?"

I turned and leaned in fumbled with my keys. I got the door open and she leaned in to sling the gym bag onto the seat. I would have been proud had I not looked at her ass in those shorts, but obviously, I looked.

She looked at the car and the duct tape on the soft top. "Can we put the top down?"

"Yeah but uh..." It was still overcast, but the rain had stopped for the moment. I couldn't help but notice four guys coming around the corner. They had your classic douche-bag biker look. One was pulling a butterfly knife, one was lazily twirling a chain, one had a lead pipe that it looked like he'd picked up out of a dumpster, and the last was simply cracking his knuckles. "Are these guys with you?"

She turned and looked. "Nope, they're Heaven's Hotdogs."

That sounded so ridiculously stupid I had to ask. "What?"

"Heaven's Hotdogs." She leaned into the car and opened the gym bag. "The biker gang."

"That's the shittiest name for a biker gang I've ever heard!" They were four intimidating looking guys, but Heaven's Hotdogs? Seriously?

She stood up out of the car with a tonfa. A Tonfa is like a police bully club but Kung Fu'ed. She held the perpendicular shaft and let the length lay along her forearm with several inches of shaft exposed further than her fist. She looked to the bikers then smiled to me. "They're hardcore Christians. What do you expect?"

"That's him!" Called out the biker with a Mohawk and butterfly knife.

Gretchen smiled. "Get the car started and I'll deal with this."

"What?"

She swayed her hips as she twirled the tonfa in her hand before securing it in an under forearm grip in her left hand while sauntering toward the four men, the smallest of which had nine inches and a hundred pounds on her. She got a bit of bounce in her step and moved side to side. The guy with the butterfly knife laughed until she darted in and got his wrist with the L of her thumb and hand edge, and the elbow with her tonfa, breaking his arm twenty degrees the wrong way at the elbow.

She rolled her steps to the left past the screaming biker and jump-kicked the man with the chain just under his chin, snapping his head back. She had to jump to do it, but God she cracked it. She made Bruce Lee sounds as she hit the ground while rapping the man over the knee with the tonfa before she spun, somersaulting toward the biker with the crucifix nose ring and pipe. She came up and rammed the blunt end of the tonfa into his crotch.

She spun again and came up as the fourth man swung. It wasn't like a movie, she wasn't blocking, but dodging out of the way after every punch. I watched her whack the turds wrist with the tonfa while simultaneously kicking him in the crotch.

I watched a petite scantily woman dance around beating the crap out of four – admittedly pathetic – idiotic themed bikers, but bikers nonetheless. I guess even in the weirdest scenarios a man can sustain an erection.

It was in that moment I remembered I needed to get the car started. I jumped behind the wheel and cranked it. Like normal, it never started the first try. I glanced at the mirror and saw her crack the tonfa over a biker's head. The car roughly idled and I reached back to unzip the back window then unclasped the soft top and pushed it back.

I took my eyes from the mirror and saw two more Heaven's Hotdogs approaching from the front. Now my fighting style can best be described as inarticulate late 1800's drunken Irishman boxing. Gretchen might be all Kung Fu, but I'm not. I reached under the arm of my suit and pulled my 1911. I lifted it up and aimed over the top of windshield.

"Back the fuck off, goddammit," I barked as I got my sights on them.

The two guys stopped and hit me with very angry looks. "Hey man," The red head with gauged ears barked, "watch the blasphemy!"

I aimed the .45 five at that guy's junk. "I'll say whatever I want. I'm the guy with a gun, *goddammit*."

They gasped. "Seriously, blasphemy!"

I let my aim bounce between them back and forth as I repeated, "Goddammit, goddammit, goddammit, god motherfuckin damnit!"

"Seriously!" The biker with the crucifix face tattoo almost looked like he was going to cry.

I started to laugh but my foot fell off the clutch. The car lurched forward and died. "Goddammit." I got my foot back on the clutch and cranked the car.

In the time I'd reached down to restart the car they'd gotten closer. I had the pistol in my left hand and aimed over the driver's side mirror as I slid back into the seat. I looked up and saw the two bikers had gotten closer. One had pulled out a pair of nunchuks.

I aimed the pistol at his chest. "Can you seriously use those?"

The other biker looked to his buddy. "He's right, can you use those?"

"Sure," the guy growled and started twirling them. He held them art at arms-length and twirled them, then dropped them when he hit his own elbow. I couldn't help but laugh but to be fair, his buddy laughed too.

I felt the Miata shake and looked over to see Gretchen jumping into the passenger seat. She smiled. "We should probably go."

I looked over to her. She slid the tonfa between the seat and the door. Her smile was luminous. It wasn't the smile of a woman who had just kicked four bikers' asses with Kung Fu awesomeness.

I kept the .45 aimed to the two in front of us as I got the car going and on the road. Once we made the corner, I holstered the pistol. "So, Kung Fu?"

She laughed, and her hair started dancing in the convertible breeze. "No. I don't do Kung Fu."

"Well that shit looked like Kung Fu." Why couldn't people just accept all martial arts were Kung Fu in the common vernacular?

I shifted gears and she reached over squeezing my hand on the gearshift. "It wasn't Kung Fu. It was a mix of Aikido and Jeet Kune Do."

"Oh, well that clears that up." I chuckled then reached in my pocket pulling out my iPhone. I plugged it into the jack coming from the car radio and handed it to her. "Want to pick us some tunes?"

She grinned and started scrolling. "Do you not have a lock code on your phone?"

"No." I glanced to her and added, "Who the fuck would want to steal my shit?"

"Why not?" She looked puzzled. "It's a common security measure."

"I know I'd forget it."

"Well that makes sense I guess." She started thumbing through playlists.

"What were those assholes up to?" I checked the mirror. I didn't see anyone following us but you know what they say about paranoia... you only have to be right once for it to all be worthwhile.

"They were after you," she muttered offhandedly as she looked through the music.

"Why?" I glanced to her.

She chewed her lip, then said, "I think they think you have something."

"I do have something, a mild buzz and a hot crazy person in my car."

She smiled. "You think I'm hot? If I'm crazy, why didn't you leave me at Sharky's?"

"Yes, you're hot. In fact, I think you know you're hot. How could you miss the hot part? Think about that, and..." I gestured to my rumpled suit and skinny form, "what about this makes you think I get attention from people like—" I gestured to her form sitting on the leather seat next to me. "You know, you?"

She took my hand and gave it a squeeze. "That's oddly sweet."

"Yeah, well, with your level of hotness I can put up with a higher than average amount of crazy." I checked the mirror again. This time I saw motorcycles, eight of them, coming up from behind us.

"Shit."

She looked behind us. "Heaven's Hotdogs." She patted my arm excitedly and looked back at my phone in her hand. "Well that's settled then."

"What is?"

I heard the speakers in the headrest start thumbing with a steady, intense beat. The drums kicked in with the base line like the driving momentum of the incoming tide. She held the phone up for me to see, the song was Filter's *Hey Man Nice Shot,* the first song on the playlist *Car Chase Mix*.

III. Car Chase Mix

Gretchen unbuckled and turned around in the seat, leaning against the dash to watch behind us. "I'm counting eight."

"Okay, what the hell am I supposed to do about it?" I had to slow a bit to make a corner but gave it all the gas my shitty car had, trying to make space.

"Drive faster." She pulled her gym bag in her lap and pulled out a leather pistol holster with rounds in loops and two low slung bonded ivory gripped silvered Colt Single Action Army pistols.

I look at them then up to her pretty dark eyes. ".45 colts?"

She smiled. "Close. Custom .357's."

"You do cowboy action shooting?" I couldn't help but imagine her in a cowboy hat; a black one with a silver band. Trading out the combat boots for cowboy boots and spurs. Why was that working for me?

She pulled one of the pistols from the holster and twirled it like a pistoleer. God, even that was hot. “Yep.”

She thumbed back the hammer of the pistol and started aiming behind us. I glanced in the mirror and even with objects appearing closer than they are, they were still too far back for pistols. She lowered the aim. “Not yet.”

“What? Too far for the shot, or not yet for starting a goddamned running gunfight in the middle of the city when technically they’ve done nothing but get their asses kicked?”

She cocked her head to the side confused for a moment. “That’s true.” She turned around and slid back into the seat. “I didn’t think of it like that.”

“How were you thinking about it?”

She smiled. “That they were following us, gonna try and kill us and things were going to start off bad and degenerate from there.”

“Well maybe they’re not following us.” I made a left hoping that maybe this was the case, but they made the turn too. “They’re still following us.”

She bit her lip. “I’m trying to figure out an alternative to shooting them, but I don’t think we’re gonna out run them.”

“I got a shitty car. I get that.” The sound of the valves clattering didn’t hurt articulating the point.

“No. I mean,” her head cocked to the side, “what if you’re right. What if they’re not after you? Then I kicked their asses for no reason. I mean, no reason whatsoever.”

“Well they do have the fuckin dumbest Motor Cycle Club name ever.”

She smiled and patted my hand on the gearshift. “They do. I don’t feel bad about it now.” She glanced behind us, causing her raven hair to whip around. “You do have the dumbest club name!”

The song changed from *Hey Man Nice Shot* to Motley Crue's *Kickstart My Heart.*

She laughed, “This is a good mix.”

“Thanks, I’ve been saving it for a car chase.” I couldn't help but smile.

“So that’s why it’s the Car-Chase mix?”

I shrugged.

"What other mix's do you have?" She started looking at the phone to scroll through the playlists. "You have a Gun-Fight Mix?"

"Who doesn't have a gunfight mix?"

She laughed. "I got one too. But believe it or not, a lot of people don't. Well, most people don't."

"Want to know a secret?"

"Hit me," she said with a smile.

"*Hey Man Nice Shot* and *Kick Start My Heart* are the only two songs I got on both the Gun-Fight and Car Chase Mix's."

She laughed. "Well they're good selections. What's on the gun-fight mix?"

I smiled. "AC/DC's *Shoot to Thrill*."

She bounced in the seat and grabbed my forearm. "God I love AC/DC!"

I couldn't keep the smile from my face. "They're the greatest band ever, right?"

"No, you're absolutely right!" She chuckled as she watched behind us.

I looked over to her. "Wait, say that again."

"What? That you're right?"

"Yes. That part."

She smiled. It gleamed like the light reflecting off her pistols. "Well, you are right. Why did you want that repeated?"

"Oh, that's just the sexiest thing a girl can say," I said with a smirk.

She grinned and twirled the pistol in her hand. "Why are you cool to me?"

I glanced at the mirror and they were closing. I whipped the wheel and turned down a one-way street, the wrong freaking way. Four of the eight followed us. "What do you mean?"

"You're not handling this the way I'd expect."

"What do ya mean?" I whipped around a swerving car who was confused by my driving.

"Most guys wouldn't be cool with taking a ride with someone they just met carrying martial arts weapons and pistols in a gym bag. So why are you being cool?"

"Because I want to have sex with you." Normally I would lie, but idiot Christian bikers were chasing us, and my mom had been buried earlier this morning, and I had a lack of sleep. But really it was the Christian Biker thing.

The song changed to Rammstein's *Du Hast*.

She smiled. "Oh, this is a great song." That was about as good a reaction as I could imagine to the admittance of carnal desire. "So we're in agreement, they're after us because either they're after you, or they're mad you pulled a gun on them."

"No." I shot her a dirty look. "No, they're pissed because you kicked four of their ass's."

I cut a right onto another road, this time I was going the right way. I heard the engines roar behind us and one of the motorcycles pulled ahead. The passenger side mirror next to Gretchen exploded and the windshield on her side turned into a spider web of broken glass. I looked back and saw the biker on the passenger side holding a sawed off double barrel.

Gretchen leaned between the passenger and driver's seat, arm extended and the .357 roared. Her round hit the bike along the tank but it didn't penetrate. It ricocheted and hit the biker in the thigh. He screamed and swerved and crashed into a parked car.

"Goddammit... your gonna give me tinnitus!" I yelled annoyed as I could, hearing the ringing in my ear.

She laughed playfully. "You'll be Sterling Archer!"

I laughed and couldn't help but yell, "DANGER ZONE!"

I looked to the right and saw the biker pull close and draw a revolver. I swerved and hit the bike with the side of the car causing him to waver and slide and tumble.

"They shot at you first," I said. "See they're pissed you kicked their ass's."

"Maybe they're just shitty shots?" she offered helpfully.

She fired again, slashing the front tire of one of the bikes. The bike tumbled to the road.

"Are you aiming at them or the bikes?" I glanced at the rearview mirror. There were five bikers left and grouped together.

"I'm aiming at the bikes right now. Should I start shooting at them?" She thumbed back the hammer and aimed.

"Well, dead in a bike crash is as dead as bullet-dead, right?"

She leaned back against the dash and scratched her forehead with the barrel of her revolver. She had filed the front sight post off. This would give her a faster draw. Even without it she was a good shot. "Well that's an interesting thought."

"Huh?" I jerked the wheel making a corner and scraping a mailbox taking it over.

"I mean, I never thought of it that way. But I guess you're right. Dead is dead."

I watched the bikes getting closer. "Where the fuck are the cops?"

"What do you mean?" she asked as she cracked off another round.

"I mean, this is a straight up car chase with a biker gang. I mean you're shooting in the middle of the city. Where the fuck are the cops?"

She shrugged, then shot. I shook my head. This kind of thing doesn't happen. In reality, bikers didn't chase cars through a town. Car people didn't shoot at bikers. If your trying to bring down a car, this sure as hell isn't the way to do it. There are three ways to stop a car in a chase. First, you take out the driver. I was really hoping they didn't go for that option. The second was taking out the engine block. The third was taking out the tires.

It was like these guys were idiots doing what they thought they were supposed to do as opposed to knowing what they're doing.

"Hey, on my signal, open your car door," I growled.

She smiled and turned around in the seat. "Oh, this is gonna be awesome!" She put her foot on the door and grabbed the handle. Her eyes shined as she looked over to me. I grabbed the handle on my door. As weird as it was, I smiled and laughed as I yanked on the door handle. I slammed on the break and the car skidded to a stop and the momentum yanked the door open.

Gretchen braced against the dash as the doors flew open. One motorcycle passed wide to the driver's side, two roared to the passenger side. The sound of crashing metal screeched as a motorcycle slammed into the driver's side door, tearing it off and sending the bike and biker tumbling down the road. Another bike slammed into the passenger door. The biker flew from the bike and the motorcycle spun down the road. The passenger door didn't come off but dangled off one hinge.

Gretchen laughed and kicked her feet excitedly on the dash. "God that was awesome!" The music changed to Judas Priest's *Breakin' The Law*. She kicked the dash and it exploded as the airbag deployed. I watched her knees press up around her head.

I couldn't help it. Yes, I laughed as I watched her nearly bend in half. I reached in my pocket and whipped out my Gerber. I flipped it open and pulled out the knife blade, stabbing the air bag. She managed to get her legs down.

I looked up and saw three of the bikes turning around. I groaned and got us in gear and turned down a side street giving it as much gas as the stressed-out engine could handle. Sparks flew as the broken door drug along the road.

"You are fucking flexible!" I yelled over the sound of grinding metal and clanging engine.

"I'm a stripper. Did you see that? That was movie crap!"

She started pulling shells from her belt and replacing her spent cartridges. "Why don't you have any hip hop on the Car Chase Mix?"

"I'm not a huge hip hop fan, what do you suggest?" I asked only as a way to keep my mind off the surreal tableau of insanity that was currently surrounding me.

She thought for a moment. "Ludacris's *Move Bitch*?" Gretchen didn't wait for me to reply before she held onto the seatbelt and started kicking the broken door. The door bounced and dragged and finally tore free and skidded into a park car. She turned around watching behind us again.

I looked up to check the rearview mirror two seconds before it exploded as a 9mm slug tore through the windshield. Gretchen cooked off a few rounds as I heard rounds pinging into the trunk and shattering my taillights.

For a second it felt like I got punched in the left shoulder. Then I realized it was a round that ricocheted off the body, punched through my seat and into my left shoulder. "FUCK!"

Gretchen emptied her cylinder and started reloading as she leaned over and poked her finger in the hole of my suit and shoulder.

"FUCK!" I jumped in my seat. My shoulder freaking hurt and I could feel my shirt getting wet with blood.

"Hey," she called out into my ear over the sounds of the chase. "You've been shot."

"No fuckin shit!" I barked, but I kept us on the road.

"You should get that looked at." Her voice was both helpful and annoying all at the same time.

"Really?" I looked over to her and even with a bullet in my shoulder she was pretty. Her breath smelt like Wintergreen Life Savers.

The car drifted and started scraping along a few parked cars. I felt a thud in the car and looked back seeing a Heaven's Hotdog hanging on to the trunk and crawling up. Gretchen was reloading. I took my foot off the gas and turned to grab him. I punched him in the face and he came around punching at me. Gretchen grabbed the guy's forearm dragging the fist down before he could land the shot.

The pain in my shoulder, the trashed car. I was fuckin pissed.

I drew back and felt something hard and solid in my hand. I thought it was Gretchen handing me the tonfa behind my back. I swung bringing the weapon around. It was a short, Spartan Xiphos style sword. It was like my hand was wreathed in fire, the same fire that formed the blade. The biker's right arm and head came off with one swipe of the sword. The corpse fell off the back of the car and tumbled in the middle of the road. Gretchen grabbed the arm and threw the it away before she tossed the head which sat on the trunk staring idiotically at us.

"I knew it!" She laughed as she looked in awe at the sword of fire in my hand. "See, they are after you and not me!"

The Car-Chase Mix changed to Ram Jam's *Black Betty*, and that was when the car crashed into a telephone pole.

IV. Lawyer Client Privilege

Ever have that moment just before you open your eyes and think: *God let it have all been a nightmare*? Deep down I knew I wasn't that lucky.

I opened my eyes.

I don't know how long I was out, but it couldn't have been long. My back hurt where the airbag exploded and forced me into the seat. Next to me Gretchen was unconscious in the passenger seat. Even as she sat knocked out with her hair astray, she looked amazing.

I heard voices even though they were bleary. I looked around and saw people milling around the car. I reached down to the radio and found the plug that lead to my iPhone. I un-jacked it and slid it into the inside pocket of my suit jacket, then I reached under the seat and found my emergency flask and slid it into my other jacket pocket alongside my regular flask. I unbuckled my seat belt and pulled myself out. I stumbled but grabbed the wrecked car to steady myself. I managed to get to the trunk and pulled it open grabbing a half roll of duct tape and sliding it over my wrist.

I stumbled around the car and started dragging Gretchen from the passenger seat. I knew I should simply bolt and get out of there... I knew that like I knew we lived in a heliocentric world. Someone once said, "Know Thyself." But they probably said it in Greek or Latin or some weird language. But just because I couldn't spell it in the original context didn't mean it wasn't a true and smart thing, a fact like gravity. Well, I knew and know myself and this is what the facts were and are. Guys like me don't have girls like Gretchen fall in their lap. Guys like me don't have girls that look like Gretchen, who kick ass like Gretchen, who have good tastes in music like Gretchen, walk through the door.

I should have run. Instead I pulled Gretchen from the car and did it without copping a feel. I never thought of myself as a gentleman, but maybe with her I wanted to be?

I leaned in and got an arm and her crotch around my shoulders. I stood, lifting her up in a fireman's carry. I bit my lip as I felt her weight dig into my wound and wondered how this was adding to the damage of the bullet. I didn't walk down the road but instead headed down the sidewalk, turning into the first alley I came to. She really didn't weigh a lot; the worse thing was the rounds on her pistol belt digging into me as I carried her and the previously mentioned bullet in my shoulder.

"You can put me down now," she mumble-groaned on my shoulder. I stopped and let go of her leg and she slid down my back till her feet touched the ground.

"Where are we?" she asked as she leaned back against the side of a dumpster.

"An alley, a couple hundred yards from the car," I told her before sucking in a deep breath.

"What happened to the car?" She reached down to one of her belt pouches and took a hair band out, tying her hair back. There was a smear of blood on her thigh, but that was my blood, not hers.

"We fuckin crashed."

She looked up at me, grinning. "We? You were the one driving, asshole."

Despite everything, I felt myself smirk. "You don't have to be a bitch about it." I pulled out my pocket flask and unscrewed the top and took a long pull of scotch. I held the flask out for her.

"Sorry." Her voice was apologetic, but her smile was surprisingly carefree. Our fingers brushed as she took the flask and took two long tugs from it. She handed the flask back. I could hear her small laugh.

"What's so funny?" I asked, as I reached over to take the flask back.

She looked me over and cocked an eyebrow. "Your suit says consignment shop sale, but your scotch is definitely top shelf."

I winced as I leaned back, and my shoulder rested against the wall. I took another pull from the flask before screwing the cap on and putting it in my pocket. "I like my Scotch old enough to get drafted and die for my country."

She laughed. In the distance we could hear sirens. "We should go."

I wrapped my good arm under her right arm, helping hold her up as we started shuffling down the alley. She wrapped her arm around my waist.

She looked up concerned. "We need to find someone to look at your shoulder but I think a hospital is out. They'll be watching those."

I could feel my teeth grinding. "Who are *they*?"

"At a minimum, the Heaven's Hotdogs. But now that it's clear you have it, everyone is gonna come after you." Her voice was all business at that moment.

"Have what?"

"Nick, you have the Fiery Sword." She looked and sounded serious even if what she was saying was bat-shit crazy.

"Look, I dunno what the hell happened back there, even though I did remember lobbing someone's head off."

She stepped close and held my cheek in her hand; it was gentle, oddly reassuring. "Nick, you have to trust me on this."

"Fine," I conceded. "Say you're right, what now?"

"I don't know," she said before pausing. She looked up and down the alley. "We need to get somewhere safe and get your shoulder taken care of."

I reached in my pocket and got my phone. "I know some guys." I started dialing. I slid my right arm around her hip to both help steady each of us and it was as good an excuse as any to get closer. We began slowly limping down the alley.

The phone rang and I heard a cheerful voice answer the other end. "Nick?"

"Hey, Tessa." I grimaced as I felt my bloody wet shirt rub against my shoulder. "Phil around?"

"Sure, let me get him." You could hear Tessa smiling on the other end of the phone. She and their kids were always so delightful. Tessa had been thrown out of Ireland in her 20's, but that was another story.

I heard the shuffling sounds of phones being passed around and then heard the upbeat voice of Phil come on the line. "This business or pleasure?"

"Business," I told him sadly.

I heard Phil sigh. "Okay, hit me."

"Running car chase gunfight?"

"Crap," he paused. "Anyone dead?"

I thought of lopped-off head guy. "Yes."

There was a pause long enough that I stopped to see if my phone had dropped the call before I heard Phil mutter. "You need to call a lawyer."

"I did." That seemed obvious.

"You need to call your lawyer," Phil rebutted.

"You are my lawyer."

"No," he continued judiciously, "I'm a guy you were in the army with who happens to *be* a lawyer and whose wife and kids adore you. That doesn't make me your lawyer."

"It kinda does." I'm usually not one for emotional blackmail, but desperate times and all.

"No, it doesn't." He seemed more adamant than normal but to be fair, this was a much stickier wicket than what I normally dropped on him.

"Okay, Phil, put Tessa on the phone and let's see if you're my lawyer."

He paused again. "That's low."

I had to press on. I was bleeding, after all. "So you got any ideas?"

"Are you alone?"

"No, I got a girl with me."

His tone perked up again. "Well, that will make Tessa happy. Who is she?"

"A stripper I met."

"At Titanium Lighting?"

"Sharky's."

"Ewww." I couldn't fault him having that reaction. "Was she in the car with you?"

"Yeah." That seemed a stupid question for one of the smartest guys I knew.

"Well, get the car disinfected." Now he sounded like he was lecturing one of his daughters about why we shouldn't stick paper clips in outlets, not that his daughters would ever do that anyway.

"The car is trashed and dumped against a telephone pole on Gruber Ave." We stopped before leaving the alley. Gretchen dug through a dumpster and came out with a stained canvas grocery sack with a broken strap. She pulled off the pistol belt and stuffed it in the sack, holding it closed before we could step out onto a sidewalk.

"Nick, seriously, if you were ever going to listen to me, now is the time. You need to go turn yourself in to the cops." I really wished Phil had sounded flippant and not concerned about all this... that would have been easier.

I looked to Gretchen and her dark eyes met mine. I knew whoever was after me was after her. I'd only known her for an hour and a half, but there was something. It was more than the way she looked. It was more than the allure of watching her handle herself in action. I felt alive for the first time in a long time. It was the first time in a long time I didn't miss Fallujah. It wasn't the action of a war zone you miss, it's the clarity of purpose. In Fallujah, I never woke up and wondered, where am I and what am I doing here? There, I just knew. It wasn't the bikers chasing us, it wasn't the car chase, it was her. For the first time I could remember in an age, even if I couldn't explain why, I knew exactly where I was and what I was doing.

She smiled.

My eyes were locked to hers. "I can't do that, Phil."

Phil was quiet for a good minute. "Nick, as your lawyer I'm not telling you Tessa picked me up from work yesterday, so my car is still at the office. I won't see that car until tomorrow, so I can't really report it stolen. And even if it *were* stolen, I don't think I'd ever see the fifteen hundred hidden under the spare tire. Luckily, you weren't there when I put the hide key on the car."

"Your too good a guy to be my friend, Phil." I knew exactly where the hide key was because I was there when he put it in the magnetic case and stuck it under the bumper. What kind of guy does that? How could a guy like me have friends like that?

"Good luck, Nick." Phil hung up the phone.

I slid it back in my pocket and looked to Gretchen. I glanced down at her thigh and tore the right sleeve of my cheap shirt off and handed it to her. I gestured down to her right thigh. "Sorry, but it looks like your ragging pretty bad."

She looked confused as I slung my jacket off and hung it on the corner of a dumpster. She looked down and saw the blood smear on her thigh. She chuckled and reached down, scrubbing the blood away as best she could. "Good catch. What did your friend say?"

"Enough." I tore off my other sleeve and wadded it up. I slung my arm painfully out of my shoulder holster and let it dangle off my right arm. I pressed the torn sleeve to my wounded shoulder and tore off strips of the duct tape to hold it in place. I watched her hair dangle as she continued scrubbing her thigh.

"How did you find me?" he asked.

"I told you I'm part of an organization."

"Yeah, a bunch of Latin I don't understand. Go on." I got my jacket and shrugged it back on before adjusting it over my shoulder holster. It was good that it was black, it hid the growing bloodstain on my back.

"They trained me and the task they gave me was to bring you in. They have a whole file on you. At least four other operatives were out trying to find you."

"Why?"

"Because of the sword made of fire that you used to kill the biker just before the crash. Someone wants it. Someone powerful with reach."

"So, why are you following me instead of trying to take me in? You've not even suggested going anywhere."

She finished scrubbing and carelessly tossed the rag down on the ground. For the first time in all this, I saw fear on Gretchen's face. It was still attractive, but not as pleasant. "I'll be honest. I don't know."

"You gotta do better than that."

She stepped back and leaned against the wall. "You're right." She gestured to the end of the alley. "You're probably safer without me, Nick. Go."

"What?" I figured she'd abandon me at some point, but not right after some weird, surreal car chase.

"Go. Don't let them catch you. Don't let any of them get you, Nick." Tears were actually welling in her eyes. "Leave me here and go."

I stood there. I thought about reaching under my jacket and touching the 1911 in my shoulder holster... everyone has a security blanket, right? I didn't. She was right. I should go. I didn't know her motives or her reasons for sticking with any of this.

I stepped close and slid my right arm around her, holding her steady to my side. I started walking toward the end of the alley.

She looked up to me confused. "Why?"

My eyes locked to hers. Her eyes were dark and deep. I fell in and it was okay. I gave her the simple, profound, and unfiltered truth. "Girls like you leave guys like me. Guys like me don't leave girls like you."

She squeezed her left arm around my waist and smiled.

V. Jam-Her

I had enough cash in my pocket to get us a cab. I thought about heading to Phil's car, but I didn't follow through. I wasn't going to fuck a buddy unless I had to. In the cab, Gretchen acted provocatively enough that the driver was never going to remember me. He dropped us off in front of a two-story building in a strip-mall. Before us stood a Dry Cleaners whose sign was in four Asian languages before it became English. The extent of the English on the sign was "1-Hour $$ Agreeable."

Next door to it was a nail salon with a mix of old and young Asian women who were probably hated their job, but seemed happy enough through the window.

We walked around the end of the strip-mall and past a dumpster. We were slow going up the stairs. We ended up taking two breaks. When we got to the door Gretchen leaned against the rail and I leaned against the wall then pushed the buzzer.

The door was sturdy and thick, and bolted with a full half-inch of steel plating, so really there was not any real reason to bang on it. I hit the buzzer again. After a moment I heard the speaker crackle.

"Go away."

I went to push the speaker button to talk but it was busted. "Goddammit," I muttered and pushed the buzzer again and simply kept holding it. It took a minute, but I finally heard the seven locks disengage and the door crack open.

"Nick?"

I looked through the cracked door. "Yeah. I need a hand, buddy."

"I'm kinda tripping balls right now, man."

"Right, well..." I tried to smile and turned around and tugged down my jacket. "I'm kinda fuckin shot."

The door closed and I heard three chains disengage. When I say chains, I don't mean home door chains, I mean real logging chains. The door finally pushed open as I turned around and straightened my jacket. Gretchen moved back to my side and we held each other up.

He stood around 5'6 and wasn't the brick shithouse he was when I met him fifteen years ago, but he'd not gotten fat, either. His hair was wild, but his beard was trimmed. I could forgive the hair, he was tripping balls after all. He was wearing a stained wife beater from a restaurant there in the strip mall and had white boxers with red and pink hearts on them. He had heavy wool socks on his feet. In his left hand he was holding three Tacito's between his fingers like he was a strange, Mexican food Wolverine.

His eyes locked on Gretchen and slowly lashed up and down her petite form. His smile was appreciative. "Well hey. I'm Jammer." He held up his left hand with the Tacitos. "Could I interest you in a deluxe Tacito? Pan fried, not microwaved."

Gretchen cocked her head to the side and smiled. "Oh, that's so sweet. But no thank you, Jammer."

Jammer lowered his hand and looked to me. "Is she real or am I more fucked up than I thought?"

"She's real enough, buddy." I stepped forward and Jammer moved to the side Gretchen and I slid past. It was a small room, adorned with nothing except another heavy armored door. Jammer didn't usually work from home but when he did, he wasn't stupid about it.

"How do you two know each other?" Gretchen asked so cheerfully that it must have been faked.

Jammer shut the outer door and started rearming the locks and chains. "We were in the army together."

Gretchen looked between the two of us. "Neither of you look like you were in the army."

I chuckled without really opening my mouth. Jammer looked offended. "Well you look like a stripper."

"I *am* a stripper." It didn't come out as bragging, just a statement of fact. It was weird hearing someone admit to it so perky and without any shame. Usually there was shame or quantification like "right now" or "for now." Not with Gretchen.

Jammer smiled. "Where at? Titanium Lightening? Howdy's Boobs and Booze Joint?"

"Sharky's."

Jammer's eyes narrowed suspiciously. "Bullshit. What's your name?"

"That's where we met," I grumbled. Jammer had been working the safe dial on the armored door but stopped and spun it resetting it.

"I'm Gretchen." She smiled and held out her right hand.

He glared at Gretchen accusingly. "Whom do you work for? The Cops? DEA? It's low using a simpleton like Nick to get to me!" Jammer was the only person I knew who could consistently get *who* and *whom* correct.

The guy clutching Tacitos in his boxers calling me a simpleton was kind of the low point of my day. I'd gone to my mom's funeral, crashed my car and been shot... but that was the worst.

"Dude." I tried to sound calm, but I was tired, sore, shot, and slowly bleeding. "Calm down."

"She's not a stripper, Nick!" Jammer was yelling now, basically historically. "Her name's not even right!"

"My name?" Gretchen asked cautiously.

Jammer nodded rapidly. "Strippers are named after virtues or precious material you'd make jewelry out of!"

"What?" Gretchen's jaw dropped in confusion.

"He's actually right." She looked at me accusatorially as I looked down to her. "Strippers are named Gold, Opal, Sapphire, Jade..."

"Jades are always strippers," Jammer said, nodding in agreement.

"Charity, Chastity..."

"Chastity's are always whores." Jammer smiled.

"Gretchen's a librarian's name." I offered.

She shot me a dirty look at that one..

"But not a porno librarian," I continued, "a regular librarian, like a research librarian at a high school. But not a shitty inner city high school, more like an upscale high school for upper middle-class kids whose parents want the best for their kids, but can't afford to send them to private school." Jammer was nodding his head so enthusiastically I was afraid the bobble-head he had become was possessed.

It was quiet for a moment before Gretchen said in a slow, deliberate and cold voice, "Gretchen, in Greek, means pearl."

Jammer looked up and chewed his lip before raising his hand to take a bite of his Tacito. "Okay, pearls make jewelry. Okay, you're a stripper. But this doesn't explain why you're with him." He poked at me with the hand holding his food.

She sighed. "I'm a member of the *Qui Ordinis Fratrum et Sororum Germanica Domus Sanctae Mariae* in Jerusalem, *et in umbra*. I was sent to find Nick."

Jammer leaned back against the door and reached down to scratch his junk through his boxers with his non-Tacito'ed hand. "You're one of the Teutonic Knight's Sisters in Shadow?"

I looked to Gretchen and saw her face take on a confused shadow for the first time. "You've heard of us?"

Jammer nodded. "I read about you in the Akashic Record." He then took another bite of his literal fingerfood, killing the middle one. He went from Tacito Wolverine to Tacito X-23.

"You've read the Akashic Record?" Gretchen sounded as skeptical as I must have sounded to most of the things she's said so far that day.

Jammer nodded and took another bite as his eyes wandered along a crack in the paint on the wall.

"What the fuck is the Akashic Record?" I asked, raising an eyebrow.

"It's a record of everything. Thoughts, actions... but it doesn't exist on this plane; it's on the ethereal plane." Gretchen was looking at Jammer with a mixture of confusion and accusation.

Jammer's eyes were following a crack in the wall.

I reached over and nudged his shoulder. "Jammer..."

"Oh." He blinked and looked back to us. "No, the Akashic Record is a thing on the internet. It's like Wikipedia, but with cool shit."

"The Internet?" Gretchen asked.

Jammer nodded. "Well, not the regular Internet. The weird Internet where the scary porn lives and people go to hire hit men and stuff."

"Wait." I knew what I wanted to say, but didn't know how to say it. In other words, I didn't know what to say. "So she really is in a secret society? She's not crazy?"

Jammer Pfft'ed. "The Teutonic Knights aren't really secret."

"They kind of are now," Gretchen mumbled.

"They weren't in the Crusades, but what the fuck have they done since then?" I asked.

Jammer shrugged. "Well there was the Northern Crusade." His eyes started to wander out of focus again.

"Jammer." I spoke slowly and he slowly looked back to us like he'd forgotten we were here. "I'm bleeding, dude. Want to let us all the way in?"

"Oh yeah." He smiled and turned back to the safe style door spinning the dial.

"So," Gretchen asked calmly and oddly librarian-ish. "What kind of name is Jammer?"

"A nickname."

She giggled. That was cute. "I figured that. How did you get it?"

He turned the dial and then started pulling the heavy door open. "Well, originally it was *Jam Her*. You know..." he started making repetitive thrusting motions with the Tacito hand.

"I think I get it." She smiled, and it weirdly seemed genuine.

"Yeah," he continued, "but Jam Her was just too confusing for people to text or email or instant message or stuff, but people liked calling me Jam Her so they just started calling me Jammer."

"What's your real name?" Gretchen squeezed my waist with her left arm as we started shuffling forward as Jammer pulled open the heavy door.

"Uh..." Jammer chewed the corner of his mouth. "You know it's been a long time since anyone called me anything but Jammer."

"Mike." I interjected. "Your name is Mike Bro."

"Oh yeah." He smiled and bit into the tacito.

Jammer lived in a loft that spanned the top of both the laundry and the nail salon. He had large windows over the front wall and each pane of glass had a sex toy duct-taped to it. He had office cubical walls in places to make the illusion of rooms. Behind one was a bed, behind another was a make shift office. He had a kitchen area; it contained a table with several empty take out containers and pizza boxes. Against another wall were large, substantial glass front cabinets with pill bottles. Lots of pill bottles. In front of the cabinets was a professional medical exam table and lights. It was covered with that crisp butcher style paper they keep on tables in doctor's offices.

"So, what do you do for the Sisters in Shadow?" Jammer asked as he shut the safe style door.

"Just a lot of training and stuff." She and I leaned against a pillar.

Jammer asked, "Nick and I have training. What kind of training do you have?" I'll be honest, I was curious too.

"Well, I do Jeet Kune Do and Akiedo. I'm all right at Cowboy Action pistol shooting. I'm an expert acupuncturist and Reiki—"

Jammer laughed. "Reiki! Why haven't you fixed Nick's fucked up shoulder then."

She smiled sweetly. "It doesn't quite work like that."

Jammer grunted and went to the fridge, pulling out some beers. "Where did you study that stuff?"

"At the Iga-ryu." She reached up and brushed the backs of her fingertips across my cheek, causing me to look down into her pretty olive face. "You hanging in there?" she whispered.

I nodded and heard a beer bottle bounce on the floor. "The Iga-ryu?" Jammer asked.

She nodded, "Yep."

"You're a goddamn ninja?" Jammer sounded idiotically excited.

"What?" I asked. The conversation had gotten away from me.

"Iga-ryu is where they train Ninjas, dude." Jammer seemed as thrilled as a kid on Christmas.

Gretchen seemed to weigh her answer in her mind before shrugging, nodding, and liltingly answering, "Yeah."

"You're a ninja?" I asked in disbelieving amazement. My shoulder hurt like hell, but I could still be skeptical, curious, and intrigued all at the same time. Multitasking done right.

She looked up to me with a look of apprehension

"That is awesome!" Jammer jumped before bending down to pick up the dropped bottle. He then looked at the three beer bottles. "I'm not sure which one I just dropped."

"Mike, sweetie." Gretchen said slowly. "Can we help Nick out? Do you know someone who can help him?"

Jammer nodded. "Yeah, me."

"You?" She sounded skeptical, but I could understand that.

"Yeah," I said, nodding. "We were in the 82nd but then Jammer went to Special Forces and became an 18D, a Special Forces Medic." I sounded like a proud papa. "I don't go to doctors, I go to Jammer."

Jammer sat the beers down and crammed the last of the Tacitos in his mouth. He chewed and made rotating motion with his hand like he was trying to buy time. Then he swallowed. "Okay, so what's wrong?"

I grimaced. "Been shot, Bro."

"Oh, shit, that's not cool." Jammer stumbled and tripped over his own feet. He hit the floor hard. He shook his head and pulled himself to his feet. "Well, let's see what's up."

"You sure you're okay?" Gretchen asked as he stumbled again.

"Yeah, I just dropped some acid right before you guys got here. I'll be fine." Jammer clapped his hands together. "Let's do this!"

VI: Free Healthcare on Acid

You never imagine taking your jacket off hurting, but it does when you got a bullet oozing blood from your left shoulder. My sleeveless shirt was stuck to my shoulder as I shambled over and fell on Jammer's examination table. I fell on my chest and my left leg was dangling over the side and I had to bite my lip hard to keep from yelling. Normally, I wouldn't have minded and let the yelling happen. I am A-OK with yelling. But I fell on that examination table and thought of Gretchen, and that kept me from screaming.

Jammer walked over and leaned in looking at my shoulder, then he took my dangling leg and lifted it up to the table.

"There you go buddy." He sounded like he was talking to a puppy who was afraid of jumping up onto the bed and needed encouragement. I guess a normal person might be offended, but I knew how much Jammer liked puppies, so I took it as a sign of his affection for me. Then again, who doesn't love puppies?

Well... me. I'm a cat person.

He patted my head, or petted. Probably petted. “Hey Gretchen. It’s Gretchen, right?” He looked up at her.

“Yes.” She came to the other side of the table and put her hand on my right shoulder and stroked my hair. Stroked or petted? Probably stroked, she didn’t strike me as dog person. Or maybe I was reading into that.

Jammer walked over to his bar and poured a stiff finger of Lagavulin 16. He carried it over to one of his medicine cabinets and pulled out a small lozenge that was stuck on the end of a stick. He unwrapped it and dropped it into the scotch with the small stick sticking up. He then swayed over to a set of Craftsman drawers. He opened a few until he found what he was looking for, which was a roll of duct tape then walked back to the tumbler with the lollipop and carried it over to the examination table.

He squatted and rolled back on his ass, sitting Indian style with the glass in his hand. He went to drink from it but poked himself in the cheek with the stick. “Oh.”

Jammer put the glass down and tore an inch-wide strip of duct tape about four inches long.

“What are you doing?” Gretchen asked.

Jammer looked up annoyed. “I’m sorry, are you a medical professional?”

“I am a Reiki Healer,” she answered, like she knew she shouldn’t brag about it so definitely wasn’t. “And I’m a certified acupuncturist.”

Jammer cocked his head to the side and arched his eyebrows. “So, that’s a no, right?”

I heard Gretchen sigh. “No.”

“No you’re not or no you are?” Jammer looked genuinely confused. To be fair, I don’t know if I looked it, but I definitely felt confused. Maybe it was the pain in my shoulder, or maybe it was that everyone in the room – me included, I’m not holier than thou – was a freaking idiot.

Gretchen sighed again. Oddly enough, it was a pleasant sound. “I’m not a traditional Western medical professional, if that’s what you mean.”

Jammer pulled the odd lollipop and pressed the stick to my left thumb.

I gasped as he jerked my arm then looked up. "What shoulder were you shot in?" he asked.

"My left one. The arm you're jerking, dumbass!"

He laughed. "Sorry." He took my right arm and tugged dragging me to the edge of the table so my chin was resting on the edge and the rest of my head dangled over. He took my right thumb and pressed the lollipop stick to it and wrapped the duct tape securing it. He lifted the glass and dunked the lollipop in the Lagavulin. "Okay, suck on that."

I lifted it and popped it in my mouth sucking. "God that's fuckin' awful. What is it?"

"Sixteen-year old Lagavulin, I think." Gretchen offered as she squeezed my shoulder.

"No, the fucking candy," I mumbled around the lollipop.

"Fentanyl Lollipop." Jammer smiled. "You'll suck on it till you pass out then your thumb will fall and it'll pull the Lolly out of your mouth and you won't OD or anything."

I stared at him. "Why the scotch?"

He shrugged. "You like Scotch."

Jammer looked past me to Gretchen at my shoulder. "Okay, go over there and get some sheers, cut his shirt off and I'll take his jacket downstairs to Old Lady Wu to see what she can do with it." He pulled himself to his feet by tugging the table and inadvertently – or on purpose, I don't know which – pressed his boxer covered crotch in my face. Thank God I was holding my hand up for the Fentanyl.

"Go ahead and pull his pants off too. Might as well get them cleaned as well."

I felt Gretchen's small hands start digging under me and I did the best I could to lift my hips as she undid my belt and open my pants.

Jammer laughed. "While your down there, do him a favor. I dunno how long it's been since Nick's had a Special."

"What's a Special?" Gretchen asked as she started tugging down my slacks.

Jammer laughed and made the masturbation motion. "You know, a rub and tug." He chuckled and patted my shot shoulder. Luckily the Fentanyl was kicking in. "Speaking of which, the ladies in the nail place downstairs do great rub and tugs. Cheap too! Well, not necessarily cheap, but definitely a great rub and tug for the cost conscious."

"Jammer," I mumbled around the Lolly. Gretchen had gotten my pants down to my ankles and then realized she had to get my Chuck Taylors off so she was untying them and prying them off my feet.

"Yeah, buddy."

"I don't think anyone is interested in a rub and tug." I looked up and saw the disappointment on his face. "Not today, anyway," I added and saw his smile. That smile on that goofball's face made the addition worthwhile.

Jammer dropped my jacket as Gretchen got my pants off. This fact made me wish I didn't perpetually go commando. I could feel the cool crispness of the table paper against my crotch. Jammer walked over to his cabinets and started putting stuff on a tray. I could feel myself slipping so I took the lollipop out of my mouth. "Why does this taste so bad?"

Jammer looked over and smiled. "Usually Fentanyl is for people so fucked up they won't remember, and they get knocked out quick any-who."

"What flavor is this?"

"Grape or Banana. They both equally taste like ass. That's why I dipped it in the scotch. Dip again if you need to." Jammer seemed cheery.

I dipped it back into the scotch on the floor under the table, letting it soak for a minute. Jammer came back with a tray and sat it on a nearby stand.

"I got his pants." Gretchen sounded cheerful but not annoyingly so. To be honest, her taking my pants off wasn't as exciting a moment as I'd hoped it would be.

Jammer walked over to a sink and started scrubbing up like he was a surgeon in Grey's Anatomy. "Hey Stripper, come scrub in... or are you too busy aligning his Chi?"

Gretchen patted my good shoulder and walked over and started following Jammer's lead in scrubbing. They then put on black nitrile gloves before walking back to me.

"Okay, so here is the deal," Jammer said to her as he chuckled. "I dropped some acid earlier, so I'm gonna let you do this."

Her eyebrows went up. "Huh?"

"It's cool." Jammer sounded as confident as ever. "I'll talk you through it."

"Jammer, I'm not so sure this is a great idea." Gretchen spoke softly and calmly, like a parent talking to a particularly show child.

Jammer laughed. "It'll be fine. This is like your Reiki shit, but real."

If Gretchen looked insulted by that I couldn't tell. I was still watching the end of the Fentanyl lollipop stirring in the Scotch.

"Okay," Jammer began. "First rip that duct tape off Nick's back and look at the wound. You're going to want to look close and check for bleeders. Your also gonna want to poke around and make sure no bones are shattered."

Gretchen nodded then tore it off my back in one quick go. I could feel the warmth of the blood oozing from the wound and down off my back, but because of the Fentanyl, I was blissfully okay with it.

Jammer, though still obviously tripping sounded oddly professional. "Okay, see any bleeders? How's the bones?"

Gretchen probed around a bit. "A few little bleeders."

"That's to be expected. He got fucking shot." Jammer reassured her. "How's the bone?"

"Seems to be intact." I could hear the smile in her voice, or maybe that was the Fentanyl.

"Okay, now poke your finger in the hole."

I felt pressure at the wound. It wasn't the most comfortable sensation so I popped the lollipop back in my mouth.

"What am I probing for?" Gretchen asked.

"Nothing," Jammer told her mischievously. "But when I tell the story of when a Sharky's Stripper penetrated Nick Decker, I'm gonna leave out some details for entertainment's sake."

"Jesus Christ, Jammer!" Gretchen yelled. I felt the pressure off the wound, or maybe it was the Fentanyl.

"Okay, okay." Jammer chuckled then pointed to something. "That's betadine, scrub the shit out of the whole area with that."

I felt Gretchen start rubbing around and lightly over the wound while I sucked the lollipop.

"Cool," Jammer said with approval. "Now that one is alcohol. Do the same thing with that one, but don't drink it. It's not the fun kind of alcohol." There was a pause as I felt her start scrubbing again. "I have the fun alcohol if you want."

"I'm okay right now," she assured him.

He watched as she worked. I put the Fentanyl back in the scotch. "Okay," he said, "now grab that liter bottle of water-looking stuff, then grab that fourteen-gauge needle and poke some holes in the top of the bottle." She must have been doing what he said because he continued. "Now spray it around to clean up before we go any further. It'll spray like water cause that's really all it is."

I felt the spray then the dabbing of gauze.

I heard Jammer mutter, "Okay, cool." He lifted a tool I couldn't see from the tray. "These are Curved Kelly's." He picked up something else. "This is a pair of Rat-Toothed tweezers. You're gonna take the tweezers and tug the bits of flesh around so you can work the Curved Kelly's down to the bullet."

"You sure?" Gretchen asked.

"Yeah, I'm sure."

I felt tugs and pressure.

"Okay," Jammer continued. "When you get the bullet with the Curved Kelly's, you're gonna yard that fucker out. And fair warning, it's gonna bleed like a motherfucker. I mean Nick's gonna turned into a stuck pig, so there's some Kurlex."

"It doesn't feel deep," Gretchen said, concentrating.

"Well it's probably a ricochet, so it's probably shallow." Jammer sounded like he knew what he was talking about. If you didn't know he'd been an 18D, a Special Forces Medic, you'd never believe it.

I felt a tug and warmth on my back.

"Oh shit!" Gretchen gasped.

"I fuckin told you! Use the Kurlex. Push the Kurlex and lean in on that shit with your elbow."

I now felt a lot of pressure.

"Okay," Jammer said calmly. "Now look at the bullet make sure it's intact."

There was a pause before she said: "Okay, I think it's intact."

"Eh, should be good enough. Toss it in here." I heard a clinking and then Jammer held the curved kidney bowl in front of me. "That's your bullet, buddy!" It looked like a fucked-up copper mushroom. Instead of making Mario big, it would just make him constipated. "Hollow point too, bro."

"Jammer!" Gretchen sounded a little panicked. "What now?"

"Oh, well, keep pushing with your elbow and take this." He handed her something. "Those are needle drivers and a needle with #2 Etholon. Now you're gonna use those Rat-Toothed tweezers and squeeze the hole together and sew that shit shut. But keep dabbing, cause you know... he's been fucking shot. It's gonna bleed."

There was a quiet moment as I felt Gretchen working. "How many stitches should it take?"

"Two to four. I don't care." Jammer wandered to his fridge and pulled out a bottle of Gatorade before walking back over. "Christ those are ugly stitches."

"I've never sewed before." Gretchen was defending herself. The lollipop in my mouth tasted like microwaved ass but everything was getting blurry.

Jammer laughed.

"What's funny?" Gretchen asked as she put her tools on the tray.

"Oh, well this fucker made it out of Fallujah without a scratch, and now this. It's funny." Jammer laughed again.

"What now?" Gretchen was obviously trying to change the subject. The world was getting pretty narrow and my focus was gone.

"Well," Jammer said professionally. "We pack it with Kurlex and wrap that fucker up with an ace wrap."

"That's it?" She sounded surprised.

"Yep." Jammer chuckled. "Good job." With the *good job* Jammer sounded surprised.

The world went black. The Fentanyl lollipop must have fallen out of my mouth because I didn't OD on it.

I woke up on Jammer's couch nine hours later.

Chapter VII: Vision Quest or a Conversation with Bruce Campbell

One of the greatest skills a person can learn is feigning sleep. You can learn a lot while pretending to be asleep. I found out what my ex's parents thought of me while I did this, or didn't think of me, to be more accurate. I learned a lot of gossip in the army by using this technique, so when I woke up on Jammer's couch I didn't make a big deal out of it and pretended to be asleep.

"Nick," the deep, oddly authoritative voice spoke slowly and steady, comfortingly. "We need to talk."

I decided to stick with my pretending to be asleep ploy.

"Nick." The voice sounded a little more annoyed this time. "I know you're faking."

The jig was up, but I was sticking with it anyway.

"Okay," the voice, obviously not Jammer or Gretchen, continued. "I know you can hear me so I'm just going to keep going. You've been out for about nine hours. About half an hour ago, Jammer dosed you with some mescaline. So right now, you're on a Vision Quest and you're messing it up by pretending to be asleep."

My eyes snapped open at that. "He what?"

I was lying on Jammer's couch on my stomach, my feet propped up awkwardly on the arm, but my left shoulder did feel a whole lot better. Before me and sitting on a stool was legend of the large and small screen Bruce Campbell. He was dressed in a blue Hawaiian shirt, wearing white golf pants, and was sipping on a bottle of Fireball Whiskey.

My eyes must have gone wide and my jaw dropped as my eyes fell upon the movie star. "Bruce Campbell?"

He sipped the whiskey and shrugged. "Kinda."

"Kinda?"

"Well, I'm not Bruce Campbell, but this is how you're perceiving me." Crap he had a great voice.

I sat up on the couch and started patting my pockets and realized I wasn't in my suit; I was wearing a stained pair of Batman boxers and a wife-beater.

"Are you looking for a pen to get an autograph?" Bruce asked me, half annoyed.

"Hell yes I am. We need a selfie together!" I started looking around for my phone.

He started speaking very slowly. "I'm not Bruce Campbell. I'm your Guardian Angel."

"So, why do you look like Bruce Campbell?" The boxers were too big, which made it awkward when I reached down and scratched.

"Because in my natural form I look like a big ball of light and fire and stuff, so in your head, I knew you'd recognize this as the best authority figure, and therefore possibly listen to." He gestured to himself. "Voila."

"Why don't you look like Ash Williams then?" I realized I needed to watch the *Evil Dead 2* again — that movie held up.

He leaned forward on his knees. "Because you're not the only person I Guardian Angel for. You'd think of me as Ash Williams, but she'd picture me as Sam Axe. So Bruce Campbell playing himself in *My Name Is Bruce*, is a fair compromise."

I reached out for the bottle of Fireball, which he was impolitely not offering.

He shook the bottle, "This isn't real. None of this is, you're on a Vision Quest. But it means we can talk."

"*Vision Quest* is a freaking Mathew Modine movie." I sounded incredulous because... I shouldn't have to explain that. If Bruce Campbell shows up and says he's your Guardian Angel you should be skeptical; you'd be stupid not to be.

"I know," he admitted, "and I get this isn't a sweat lodge, or spiritual or anything. But you are on mescaline, and I can't remember the native term, so vision quest will have to do."

There was an awkward pause, so I tried to nudge him along. "Okay...?"

"Okay then I dunno how much time we have, so I gotta be quick." Which seemed ironic since he was the one who had paused. He sipped the supposedly non-existent whiskey. "Nick, your mother was a demon."

"Bitch definitely, but demon?" I maintained my skepticism easily with the course of this conversation.

"Nick," He held up two fingers then three. "Your mother was the twenty-third demon kicked out of Heaven, back at the beginning of time."

"That's a fairly specific number, Bruce." I had hoped if I ever met Bruce Campbell I wouldn't be such a suspicious jackass, but we disappoint ourselves more than others ever can.

"Nick, your mother stole something. She gave it to you."

"Stole what from whom?" I didn't want this to lead to me having to have a conversation with my brother or a goddamned lawyer.

"When God expelled Mankind from the garden, he placed at the gates the Fiery Sword. Your mother stole that sword and gave it to you." He was speaking slowly, seriously. I might not have believed any of it, but he did.

"Sure," I nodded and leaned back on Jammer's couch spreading my legs inappropriately considering how large the boxer's leg holes were. "Because you know, I got swords burning all over the fuckin place. Which one is it?"

"No Nick, it's IN you, kinda. It's part of you. You've already used it." He sat down the bottle of Fireball and it disappeared as soon as it was out of his hand.

I thought back to the car, decapitating that Heaven's Hotdog. The burning sword in my hand...

"Bullshit." As much as I knew it was true I wanted an explanation. The best way to get someone to give up more info is to feign disbelief and they decide to prove themselves right. It's a pride thing.

"Okay." He leaned back as far as a person sitting on a stool could. "I know your lying, because I know you remember, and like a dude fighting a hard poop on a toilet, I'm just pushing through. So, the Fiery Sword isn't really a sword."

"Okay?" I didn't want to live in a world of real metaphors, but I think I knew that's where this was going.

"It's literally," he said, sounding pretty freaking grave, "the physical embodiment of the Wrath of God." Cue the thunder pealing and the dramatic music, I guess.

"Huh?" the *Physical embodiment of the Wrath of God*, sounded like a metaphor, not literal.

Bruce scratched his chin. "You ever go to Sunday school?"

"Wouldn't you know that, being my Guardian Angel and all?" The thought struck me that maybe the reason I had the life I've had was I was assigned the Guardian Angel I deserve.

It was his turn to chuckle. "Yes, but I'm being Socratic so just go with me."

"Yes, sir." The *sir* just felt natural.

"Don't call me sir. So you know God is a benevolent loving being, right?" For an instant he looked like he had in the last scene of Darkman, but that was just in my head.

"I'm tracking," I said and nodded in the affirmative.

"Good." He clapped his knees. "Why do you think that is?"

"I dunno... because he is?" I shrugged then reached down scratching the top of my foot. It itched.

"Nope. It's because he took all his anger and angst and pissed off-ness, aka Wrath, and made it into a weapon that he then sat in front of the Gates of Eden." He was perfectly matter-of-fact.

"So..." I don't know if I were purposefully drawing the word out or just slurring it due to the mescaline and the Fentanyl in my system. "God doesn't get pissy, because he put all the pissed off'edness on a shelf?"

Bruce smiled. "Basically."

"So where is it?" It wasn't like I was carrying around a sheath.

"That, brother, is the tough bit." He got up and walked over to the couch and wrapped his arm around my shoulder, giving me a reassuring squeeze. "It's in you. It's part of you."

"Okay?" The trip from skepticism to wherever I was going obviously traveled through Confusion-burg.

"Your mom," his tone sounded like he didn't even believe what he was saying, "stole it before the flood. You know, Noah?"

"Yeah." I wanted to say *duh* or *who fuckin doesn't?* but those both seemed rude.

"Good. She stole it just when the rain started and kept it. Then she took human form when she met your dad. When you were a kid, she gave it to you." Bruce got up and started pacing in front of the couch as he talked.

"Why?" Seemed a legitimate question.

"Because she knew one day the archangels, or the demons would find her, and they'd kill her for it." His voice was grave. It sounded like he was lamenting.

"Why?" I was starting to sound like a five-year-old.

He kneeled down in front of me, so we were eye level. "Because if either side has that Sword, everything is over."

"The fuck do you mean?"

"If the archangels get it, they'll use it to assault Hell. If the demons get it...well, I don't know if they think they can defeat Heaven, at least I don't think they do anyway, but if they have the literal Wrath of God on their side, they might try. Either way, it's not good for humanity. If either side gets that sword its Armageddon." He stood again, and my eyes followed him up. "There are three beings that didn't want that to happen. The Father, your mother, and Lucifer."

"Lucifer?" As confusing as a lot of this conversation had been, that was a curveball.

"Yeah, Lucifer." He seemed annoyed I wasn't just taking him at his word.

"Bullshit." That hadn't ever been my go-to profanity but with this conversation, it was par for the course.

"You just have to trust me on that... or ask your uncle next time you see him." Bruce sat back down. "We got one more thing to cover, and this is gonna be the most unbelievable."

"Oh, so now we're getting to the wacky bits, Bruce? Because everything up to this point has made sense?" I wished that bottle of Fireball was real.

"Look, it's about Gretchen." He really did sound grave.

"Okay, look." I leaned back. "I know she's a stripper, and crazy, and secret society ninja and all, you don't have to give me the Guardian Angel speech about not sticking your dick in crazy."

He looked to me and said completely deadpan. "She's your Soul-Mate."

"Bullshit." I repeated. I didn't mean that, it was just reflexive at this point.

"She is." He was as adamant as a stamp collector defending the authenticity of his collection while at the same time managing to not sounding like a stamp-collecting virgin.

"How the fuck do you know that?" We backtracked from Confusion-burg back through Skeptic-ville.

"Because I'm her Guardian Angel too." Again, he was perfectly deadpan. Annoyingly so.

"That must be convenient." I wanted a drink, so my sarcasm shield was pretty thin.

"Look, soulmates are weird things." Now he just sounded annoyed.

"How so?"

"Do you think it's common for soulmates to end up being alive at the same time?" He actually seemed bemused by this line of Socratic crap.

"Shouldn't they?" It seemed obvious. Maybe it was the mescaline, but I was confused.

"You'd think, but no. Alexander the Great's soulmate is a lady name Janice McAlister of Wichita Kansas, born 1963, alive right now."

"Wasn't he queer?"

"Eh, that piece of crap would put his wang in anything with two legs and would move. It's lucky he didn't meet a monkey or kangaroo." Bruce throwing his arms wide in exasperation did provide great dramatic effect for the news he was delivering. "Think about every female egg that goes un-fertilized, or every time you shot off in the shower. When Monty Python sang *Every Sperm is Sacred,* they weren't too far off the mark. There have only been four soulmates alive together in history who actually found each other."

"Who are the other four?"

He held up the four fingers of his left hand. "Adam and Eve." He lowered his pinky. "King Leonidas of Sparta and his wife Gorgo." He lowered his index finger. "Carl and Carol Prescott of Redding Pennsylvania living in the late 1800's but didn't quite crack the 20th century." He then lowered his ring finger, flipping me off I might add. "Robert and Virginia Heinlein."

"The sci-fi writer?" I loved those books, so it was nice hearing about good things happening to people you liked.

"Yep." He nodded, proud I knew who he was talking about. "You and Gretchen, are a statistic improbability, my friend."

"So why are you telling me?" The suspicious part of me was emerging. I couldn't help it. Like the scorpion on the back of the frog, I guess.

He sat back down, and the bottle of Fireball appeared in his hand again. He took a nice long sip. "Because you are stuck in the dirty middle of some bad stuff and you're going to need someone you can trust. Soulmates aren't like literature; you don't have to like each other, there's no guarantee you'll ever love each other, but your world is getting complicated quick and she can be something stable. Still it's complicated."

"How?"

He sighed and shook his head, like he was exasperated and trying to explain something simple to a really idiotic child. "Do you think because someone is your soulmate that they're going to love you? Like you? Want to be with you?"

"Well," It didn't seem like a trick question, but it felt like one, "yeah."

Bruce laughed. "No, nothing is that simple. Believe me, you can fuck this up, Nick." He patted his knee as he chuckled. "If anyone can fuck up soulmates, I'm willing to bet it'd be an asshole like you."

I nodded. "So, what do I do now?"

"There are angels, archangels and demons, and every one of them looking for you, Nick. They want the Fiery Sword and you have it." He reached over and patted my shoulder. "Right now, the only thing protecting humanity from literal Armageddon is you."

"So what the fuck am I supposed to do?" This conversation was now passing through Exasperated-Town.

"Well..." He hopped up and moved back to the stool, sitting and leaning in on his elbows. "I'm an angel, I have a side, but because I'm your guardian angel, my priority is you. I can't give you up to the archangels. As much as I want this to end, because Armageddon isn't bad for us, it's not good for you. They're coming for you. They've already started. I'm pretty sure they killed your mom, and I'm pretty sure Heaven's Hotdogs were set on you. You have to one, stay alive and two, not give them the Fiery Sword."

"If mom didn't have the Sword anymore, why did they kill her?"

"Because they couldn't find it. While she was alive she could shield you. They killed her to get to you, and to get to the Sword." It was weird hearing Bruce Campbell, a guy who had declared himself an angel sounding remorseful about the death of a demon.

"Who did it?" I could hear the iron in my voice. It was easier to accept your mom was killed in a random act than it was to hear she was killed to get to you. I felt the ire in me, and then I felt the sword burning in my hand.

Bruce looked to the Fiery Sword as it burned in my grasp. He got lost for a moment looking at it. "I know you know your mom was stabbed to death, so let me preface that I don't know for a fact the details of what happened concerning that but I'm guessing Heaven's Hotdogs were behind it. That said, I'm pretty sure by how fast they found you that they were the ones who killed your mom."

He looked directly into my eyes. "Still, for all I know there was an angel or archangel behind it."

"Fuck'em all." The Sword felt good in my hand.

"Nick, don't try and fight an angel or archangel. Others have tried, and a human has never won that fight." Bruce sounded serious and concerned. Like fighting an angel and archangel had actually been on my To-Do list and I needed convincing fighting either one was a bad idea.

"What do I do, Bruce?"

He smiled. "Do what I gotta do right now."

"And what's that?" The initial anger was gone and the sword dissipated from my grasp.

"I gotta run, brother. Good luck." And with that, like Keyser Söze, he was gone.

VIII: A Guy for That

I sat on the couch and looked to the side. Gretchen's head lay on my right shoulder and my right arm was wrapped around her. Her cheek was smooth against my skin around the strap of the wife beater. Her hair was silky and fell in light waves. It felt pretty good having my arm around her. She was wearing a Firestone Complete Auto Care work shirt belonging to someone named "Keith" by the patch. Obviously she got it from Jammer. Through the window I could tell it was nighttime but beyond that, I had no idea.

My hand shifted a bit and I realized the thumb of my right hand was a touch sticky. That was disconcerting.

I heard the TV and looked over and saw Jammer slurping noodles from a take-out carton with chopsticks. He was watching Cowboy Bebop. It took me a second, but I recognized the episode *Cowboy Funk*. The Baddie of the week was putting explosive laden teddy bears all over town and causing mayhem.

I wanted to get Jammer's attention, but I didn't want to disturb Gretchen. It was weird. Normally, I would be trying to escape but here I was, enjoying the feel of her breath washing over my arm as she rested her head in the crook between my neck and my shoulder.

She stirred as Jammer laughed. I felt her eyelashes flutter against me then she slowly looked up. She smiled, and that made me smile.

She slowly sat up and slid out of my arm.

"Jammer," I called out, tearing my eyes from Gretchen.

"Yeah, buddy." Jammer never took his eyes away from the TV.

"I got a question, and I need you to be honest with me no matter how horrible it is." Sometimes it's easy to lie to your friends. I knew I probably didn't want the truth.

"Okay, Nick, whatcha got?" He slurped loudly on more noodles.

"Why is my finger sticky?" Of all the questions I ever wanted to ask, that was not on the list.

He chewed. "Which finger?"

"Right thumb." I touched my thumb to the tip two or three times feeling the stickiness of it.

Jammer slurped some more noodles and spoke around them. "Duct tape from where I stuck the Fentanyl lollipop."

I audibly sighed. "Thank God." Let's be honest… the answer could have been way way way worse.

I reached up with my right hand and felt my shoulder. There was a bandage wrapped around it. "Why doesn't this hurt?" I slowly rotated my shoulder.

Jammer shrugged. "A combination of Fentanyl and Mescaline?"

Gretchen laughed. "After we got you laid out I realigned your Chi."

I could tell from her smile I was looking at her with so much freaking confusion. "Huh?"

She reached her fingers over my face and wiggled them playfully. "Reiki magic."

I leaned back away from the fingers, and she leaned in keeping them close, laughing.

"Get a room you two." Jammer groaned as he picked up a bottle of *Dos Equis* and sipped. "But yeah, she did her Reiki stuff after you got bandaged up."

I rotated my shoulder. "Well, that shit worked. I feel fuckin fine."

"Still say it's hooey." He slurped more then looked over. "I got your clothes from old lady Wu downstairs. She patched up your suit jacket."

"How much do I owe you?" Not that I knew where my wallet was. He laughed. "Don't worry about it. It was gratis with a Rub and Tug."

Gretchen chuckled and leaned into my side.

I felt the corners of my mouth go up slightly. "Well, let me pay for the Rub and Tug."

"I have a tab." Jammer chuckled. "So, what's your plan?"

I felt Gretchen look up to my profile and I went out of my way to not look at her. "Heaven's Hotdogs killed my mom."

Jammer, God love him, went with it. "You Vision Quest that?"

"Yeah. Like I said, my guardian angel told me." There wasn't a way to not make that sound crazy.

"I've done a lot of Mescaline," Jammer said, nodding intently, "but I've never met my guardian angel. What was he like?"

I shrugged. "Bruce Campbell."

Gretchen perked up at that.

"Dude!" Jammer almost dropped his carton. "That is awesome. I wonder who my guardian angel is?"

"Me too." Gretchen muttered with more than a hint of jealousy.

I did look to her. She was chewing on the corner of her lower lip. It was oddly adorable. "Gretchen's guardian angel is Bruce Campbell too." The second it came out of my mouth I knew I shouldn't have said it.

She smiled, and it lit her whole face up. She bounced on the couch next to me in excitement.

"Who is mine?" Jammer asked.

"Chow Yun Fat," I told him. I knew it was a lie, but Jammer lit up like a Christmas tree. His happiness made it worth it, and odds were he'd never learn the truth.

"Dude, Chow Yun Fat is freaking awesome!"

I smiled. "No shit."

"So, what's the plan?" It was Gretchen's turn to ask. I'll be honest, I'm not great at plans. I've never been great at plans. My strength has always been winging it.

"Bruce told me the Heaven's Hotdogs killed my mom," I repeated.

That sat heavy in the room. Jammer sat down his carton and grimaced. "Your mom was a worthless bitch, but I liked her."

I wasn't really sure what the appropriate response to that was. "Thanks, Jammer."

"Where do you want to start?" He asked with a foreign seriousness to his tone.

I thought on it for a bit. "We know these Christian dipshit biker assholes are armed."

"Yeah?" Gretchen asked, but Jammer was smiling. I think he knew where my mind was heading.

"Peaches," I nodded to Jammer. "We need to talk to Peaches."

Jammer stared for a moment. "You know that's never a great idea."

"Who is Peaches?" Gretchen asked.

"Peaches," Jammer said slowly, but he wasn't looking to her, he was looking to me as if he needed to explain to a kid why you shouldn't touch a hot stove. "Peaches sells guns without all that pesky democrat gun regulation or extra taxes."

"Okay, so he's a gun guy." Gretchen nodded. "And they had to get their guns from somewhere right?" She smiled. "It's a good idea."

"It would be," Jammer agreed, "except some dickhead decided he was Sam fuckin Spade and made sure Justice prevailed even though it wasn't his fucking case."

"Huh?" I felt Gretchen's hand squeeze my arm tighter as the story went on.

"That asshole," Jammer pointed to me, "decided that Peach's ex-wife deserved child support."

"Those kids did deserve child support," I interjected.

"Yeah, but how did you make it happen?" Jammer asked angrily.

"Well...." I really didn't want to answer that question.

"How did you?" Gretchen asked.

"Eh, I got some evidence and promised to keep it quiet as long as his kids got their monthly checks."

"In other words…" Jammer drew the words out.

"You blackmailed him?" Gretchen sounded suspiciously perky while making a statement that could be both declarative and interrogative.

"Well," I said as I felt the smirk tug at the corner of my lips, "blackmail is an ugly word."

"Regardless," Jammer continued, "Sam Spade here isn't the most popular bro in Peach's stable of friends."

"I'm not sure that's accurate," Gretchen said thoughtfully.

"What?" Jammer asked. "Do you know Peaches?"

"No, I mean Nick." She squeezed my arm again. "If he's a Dashiell Hammet character, I think he's more the Continental Op as opposed to Sam Spade. Spade was a good P.I., sure, but the Continental Op did shit to bring about his own form of justice."

Jammer's jaw dropped and I'm pretty sure mine did as well. Gretchen looked between me and Jammer then asked, "But if he is Sam Spade, does that make you Miles Archer and me Brigid O'Shaughnessy?" She seemed really excited by the prospect.

"Nick, tell her to stop talking crazy." Jammer sounded oddly serious.

"Make the call Jammer, set up the meet with Peaches." I didn't mean to sound as grave as I did. But we were in a weird situation. I looked over into Gretchen's large dark eyes. "Stop talking crazy."

Jammer got up and went to a drawer and pulled out a phone. He started typing a text and wandered back past one of his partitions.

"You okay?" Gretchen seemed an alloy of curiosity and concern. Her features were gorgeous. She could have been a statue in a freaking museum.

Guardian Angel Bruce Campbell told me I could fuck it up. But fuck what up? What did I want? I mean besides the obvious, what did I want? And if I wanted shit to be even more complicated, what did *she* want?

Soulmate "So," she asked, "who is Jammer, really?"

I smiled. "We were in the 82nd Airborne together, then he went off to Special Forces and became an 18 Delta."

"What's an 18 Delta?"

"Special Forces Medic. He was a Senior Team Medic. I trust Jammer more to deal with trauma than I would an emergency room."

She nodded, understanding. "Where does he get all the medical equipment?"

I chuckled. "He trades drugs for equipment and supplies from an inventory manager at the hospital."

She laughed. "So why is he setting up your meet with Peaches?"

"Well, Jammer is my 'Guy Guy.'" I must have said it matter of factly, because it drew a look of utter confusion from Gretchen.

"Huh?"

I sighed. "You know how sometimes you go X is happening, it's cool, I got a guy for that. You know?"

She nodded pensively, unwilling to completely confess to true understanding.

"Jammer is my 'Guy Guy.' If you need a gun, Jammer knows a guy. If you need a car, Jammer knows a guy. If you need a suit, Jammer knows a guy. If you need cash cleaned up, Jammer knows a guy. If you need..." I could have gone on for days, but Gretchen decided to interrupt.

She smiled. "Jammer knows a guy."

I reached over and pressed the tip of her nose. "You got it."

"Nick!" Jammer called out. "I can make a meet, but there's a catch."

"There's always a catch, so what is it?" Fuck, for once why couldn't there be a time where there wasn't a fuckin catch?

Jammer came out from behind his partition. "I figure Gretchen can be your date, though no one would believe you picked up a girl like her."

"What do you mean like her?" she growled.

"You know." He gestured up and down. "Fucking hot."

She smiled demurely. "Continue."

"Like I was saying, before being rudely interrupted. Gretchen, she can be your date. But I need one."

I sighed. "What about the Clingy Nurse?"

"Jane isn't talking to me." That seemed like a loaded statement, but I let it go.

"What about The Happy Go Lucky Whore?"

"Ah, she's working."

"What about one of the Rub and Tug gals?"

"Yeah, I go with the don't shit where you eat rule." He scratched his beard. I could tell he was leading toward something and I had a stinking suspicion I knew what.

"You're into some odd stuff, aren't you, Jammer?" Gretchen said with a laugh.

Jammer and I ignored her.

"So..." Jammer said slowly, "I need a date."

Gretchen was the only female I knew that talked to me on a regular basis that wasn't a stripper or waitress at Sharky's. Well, besides Agnes. There was no way I could throw Agnes under the Jammer bus. Agnes was my secretary. She's insanely competent, which made her suspect. Why would an insanely competent person work for me? But Agnes is the reasons the lights stay on at my office and apartment. She fishes out jobs for me, makes cold calls, and does the books. On top of all that, I'm not sure I've ever paid her. Yeah, no way Agnes gets tossed at Jammer. I couldn't afford to lose her.

"It's okay." Gretchen said now. "I can find a date for Jammer."

"Even while you're busy being Nick's date?" Jammer asked.

"I could do worse than Nick."

"Me?" Jammer chuckled. That got a laugh from me too.

Gretchen shrugged but her smile was mischievous. She reached over and nudged my shoulder. "I guess you expanded your Guy Guy entourage."

"Huh?"

"Yeah, Jammer might be your Guy Guy." She made a puckered kissy face. "But I'm your 'Find Jammer a Date Guy.'"

"It's not a whore, is it?" I whispered.

"No." That 'no' sounded pretty indignant. But I'm willing to bet Gretchen knew one or two dames who couldn't whore in the Olympics because they'd lost their amateur status.

"Is she a stripper?" I asked, because that seemed to be an obvious guess.

"No." That 'no' sounded suspect. It was like a clue in a game of Hotter and Colder. My eyes narrowed. "Define 'no."

"Okay, not a stripper but works at a strip club." Again, her tone sounded both declarative and interrogative. In my experience, anyone who was a waitress at a strip club and wasn't doing double duty as a dancer had something obviously wrong with them. But I didn't have enough info to figure out what yet.

I sighed then looked to Jammer who had a face filled with wonder and glee. "So where are we going buddy?"

He looked so happy I was curious if he was on something. He grinned a grin that the Devil himself would be envious of and filled me with dread. "Asian Karaoke."

IX: With an E-Y

The cleaners had done great fixing the hole in my suit. I got a shower and used a tube of Old Spice Original deodorant I'd left at Jammer's, then brushed my teeth with the tooth brush I'd left there too. This wasn't the first time I had crashed on his couch, but it was the first time I'd done it with a bullet wound. After the shower, Jammer rewrapped the wound but even he seemed amazed by the shape it was in. Maybe Gretchen's "Reiki Bullshit" he kept referring too was actually something after all.

I pulled on a clean white shirt and buttoned it up, leaving the last button undone. It was Jammer's shirt and oddly despite our differing builds, fit the way you'd expect a tailored shirt to fit. You couldn't tell my black slacks had had blood on them earlier in the day. I inspected the jacket and couldn't even tell that there had been a hole in the shoulder from where I'd been shot that afternoon. I slid my shoulder holster back on and pulled the 1911. I dropped the mag and yanked back the slide, ejecting the round. I held it to my nose and sniffed. Apparently Jammer had cleaned it while I'd been knocked out. He was a sweet guy like that. I put the round back in the magazine and re-fed it into the grip of the pistol. My thumb hit the release and the slide dropped. I thumbed the hammer down and eased it back into the shoulder holster, buttoning it in place. I then slid my jacket on over everything.

My feet were bare and cold on the painted concrete of Jammer's loft bathroom floor. I was about to pull open the curtain but stopped as I heard Gretchen and Jammer chatting. I'm not a gossip, but I was curious. It's not every day you find out someone is your Soul Mate and is having a conversation with your best friend.

"I know Nick from the Army." Jammer told her, more than likely answering the question *How do you know Nick*? or *How did you meet Nick?*

"I knew Nick was in the 82nd but there wasn't a lot about it in the files."

"What was in the files?" Jammer asked. "Whose fucking files?"

"I shouldn't say." Gretchen sounded regretful.

"Say anyway." I would say Jammer sounded mischievous, but he always sounded mischievous, even when he was completely sincere, which was really fuckin annoying.

"The Sisters in Shadow had a full work-up on Nick and anyone else they thought might potentially possess the Fiery Sword." Gretchen spoke slowly but her tempo increased as she continued. It was like opening the gates. If you're gonna spill secret society secrets, why not go all out?

"So, you got assigned Nick?" I could picture Jammer cocking his head and scratching his temple like a monkey.

"No." She took a long pause. "I looked through the files of Potential Wielders—"

"Do they seriously call them 'Potential Wielders?'" Jammer literally guffawed, like he was a damned character in some damned Jane Austen story.

"Yes." She sounded self-conscious.

"Sorry." He was still chuckling but stopped. "Please, continue."

"I looked through the Pot—the files. I chose Nick." She sounded almost wistful, not regretful. That was weird.

"Why the hell would anyone choose Nick?"

"I'll be honest. I don't really know... just a feeling. For everything in there, a lot of Sisters saw a scumbag or a drunk, but I didn't." There was another pause, Jammer must have been nodding or motioning for her to continue because after a moment she did. "I looked at his time in the Army. I looked at the cases he'd taken afterward as a P.I. and I think you were right, I thought he did think of himself as a Dashiell Hammett character. Not Sam Spade, and definitely not Nick or Nora Charles, but he seemed a lot like the Continental Operative. Or maybe he seemed like he was trying to live like people perceived Dashiell Hammett characters to be."

"I never read that stuff," Jammer confessed, but quickly added, "I did see the *Maltese Falcon*."

"The Continental Op was a character in some stories and the novel *Red Harvest*." Gretchen offered. "A guy who was the definition of get shit done and do bad things for the bigger good."

"I can see that, but then I know Nick, not just files." Jammer made a weird combination of consoling and one-upping at the same time.

Gretchen's voice seemed a combination of curious and playful. "Tell me about him."

"Promise it's just between us?" At this point, I felt bad about eavesdropping. But I've felt bad about a lot of things in my life, so I wasn't stopping.

"Scouts Honor."

"Well," Jammer hmmm'ed and ummmm'ed as he sought the words he was looking for. "Nick's a hero, in the worst way."

"What do you mean?" Gretchen asked, mirroring my thought of *What the fuck does that mean you asshole?*

"A car goes off a bridge, a guy dives in and drowns saving a trapped kid inside, right? He's a hero."

"I'm with you so far," Gretchen cautiously agreed.

"Well," I pictured Jammer scratching his head. "Is that moment indicative of the rest of that guy's life?"

"You mean some karmatic balance?" she offered. "Like if a pedophile gives someone a kidney, does that make up for everything else they've done?" I found myself thinking, *Did Gretchen just compare me with a pedophile?*

"Kinda," Jammer admitted. "Are we more or less our best moment? Because when things are at their worst, when the world is going to shit, no one comes though and shines like Nick fucking Decker. But the problem is the world isn't always on fire, is it? So what's a hero do in a world where you don't need hero shit?"

There was a long pause. "What?"

"That's what I'm asking!" Jammer actually gasped. "I guess become a P.I. and take pictures of married people fucking other people for better divorce settlements?"

Gretchen didn't answer, and Jammer went quiet. I decided to pull open the curtain. Jammer was wearing khaki slacks, light blue shirt, a pair of Asolo hiking boots, and a green tweed jacket with leather patches on the elbows. He was dressed like a college professor no student would fuck for a better grade to save their GPA's.

Gretchen on the other hand, looked like she stepped out of a catalogue, or PG-13 dirty magazine. She wore a dark blue dress without sleeves that clung to her like amateurly applied wall paper. It came down below mid-calf and she was shoeless at the moment, showing her dark-blue painted toenails. Next to her feet were a pair of three or four-inch shiny black heels with a strap over the front. She was pulling on her leather half-jacket that somehow made her outfit seem simultaneously oddly elegant and dangerous at the same time. She tousled her hair with her fingers.

I must have been staring because she asked, "What?" Her dark eyes met mine, drawing me in like the tractor beam dragging the *Millennium Falcon* into the Death Star.

"Uh... where did you get the dress?" It was the best I could come up with at the time. I'm usually quick on my feet, but that day, not so much.

"I grabbed it from the cleaner's downstairs," Jammer offered.

"So it's stolen?" I asked, eyebrows arching.

"Not stolen," Gretchen corrected. "Politely borrowed to be returned when we're done with it."

"She couldn't go out like she was dressed," Jammer said, as if that explained everything.

She turned her eyes to Jammer, her eyes turning from tractor beam to an accusatory pain ray-gun. "Wait, how was I dressed?"

"You know," he shrugged, "I don't know, maybe like a stripper without the ability to process shame in the human form? Like your Mom never corrected your outfits when you were a kid even when you started going to the dark side?"

I laughed, and she shot me a hurt look.

"Hey," I said holding my hands out in surrender. "I liked it, and frankly I don't think it matters what you wear. I mean, you'd be gorgeous in a brown paper bag, or anything but burlap."

"You don't think I can pull off burlap?" she asked, but the playfulness was back in her tone.

"I think it'd be too itchy." I walked over to the couch and sat down grabbing the pair of socks that had been set atop my pair of battered black and white Chucks. Gretchen bent down to pull on the pumps.

We all headed out and got into Jammer's Honda Accord. Jammer had several cars, but this was one of the more low-key; apparently that's what we were going for. I sat shotgun and Gretchen climbed in the back. She gave Jammer an address and he got us going. I know for a fact he'd never been where we were going, but Jammer was a walking, talking GPS in an awkwardly built human form.

"So, who is this date you scored me?" Jammer asked as he looked back in the rearview mirror.

"Her name is Joy." Gretchen sounded cheerful. I looked back to her and raised an eyebrow and she smiled, like the cat in a house with an empty canary cage.

"And on a scale of total dog to Maureen O'Hara in the *Quiet Man*, where does Joy fall?"

There was no hesitation in Gretchen's answering, like she'd had the answer in the chamber and was just waiting to pull the trigger on a target of opportunity. "Between Ursula Andress in *Dr. No* and Ali MacGraw in *The Getaway*."

"No shit?" Jammer probed as he glanced back in the rearview mirror again.

"Negative on the shit." Gretchen agreed. "I am shitless."

We pulled into a complex of condos and stopped in front of number 1070.

"Should I call her?" Gretchen offered.

"No, I'm a gentleman." Jammer sounded offended, and nervous. He then looked to me and whispered, "Get in the back, bro, and come on!"

I nodded and climbed out as he did. I shut the passenger door as Gretchen leaned over and pushed open the rear driver's side door.

Sitting next to Gretchen now, I asked, "So she's a waitress at a strip club?" I was watching Jammer as he waited.

"Yep, Jammer's going to love her. I can't think of anyone as fun as Joy with an E-Y." Gretchen laughed and reached over grasping my hand. Her fingers interlaced with mine.

I was amazed by the fact we were holding hands so much that I didn't notice the condo door open until I saw the tall, leggy blonde emerge.

She was over six feet, standing half a head taller than Jammer. Her blonde hair fell in golden waves half-way down her back. She wore a cream silk blouse that didn't really hide her firm C-cups, the same way her black skirt didn't hide her figure as it hugged her hips. Her six-inch heels made her even taller and leggy.

"See." Gretchen smiled. "Told you she's perfect for Jammer."

I looked to Gretchen. "Wait, what's her name?"

"Joy," she repeated with the same smile. "With an E-Y."

"Spell it." I had a bad feeling.

"J-O-E-Y, Joy."

"Gretchen J-O-E-Y is fuckin Joey!" They were moving to the car now, the tall Joy with an E-Y clinging to Jammer's arm.

Gretchen laughed. "Not since the surgery silly."

"You've hooked my best friend up with a transsexual?" I know my voice sounded disbelieving, but yeah, I was sure that's what was up.

"Post-op." Gretchen confirmed with a sure nod. "Jammer and I talked while you were out. He said, '*The hottest chick I ever saw was a dude in Thailand.*'"

My jaw dropped, but that did sound like Jammer. In fact, I'm pretty sure he'd said the same thing to me at some point. I looked out the window and Jammer was beaming as he opened the car door for Joy with an E-Y. She slid into the seat and looked back smiling to Gretchen.

"Hey Gretch, thanks for inviting me, this sounded so fun!" Joy laughed. She had green eyes that lit up when she looked at me. "You must be Nick!"

I offered my hand. "Hey, yeah... I'm Nick, Jammer's buddy." She shook my hand very lady-like. It definitely could have been firmer, but her hand was smooth.

"Gretchen usually doesn't talk about guys, but she went on and on about you!" Joy half giggled, her voice a soft soprano.

"Joy!" Gasped Gretchen. She actually sounded embarrassed.

Jammer hopped behind the wheel. "Everyone comfortable and buckled in for safety?" He was asking like he was talking to everyone, but I was sure he was just addressing just one of the car's occupants.

Joy answered as he was only looking at her anyway. "Buckled for safety!"

"Okay, off we go!" Jammer put the car in gear. "To Asian Karaoke!"

X: Asian Karaoke

Little Saigon Mega Awesome Disco Karaoke was the definition of oxymoronic juxtaposition and misappropriation. It was not in Little Saigon, there was no Little Saigon in town. It was run by a family of Filipinos, not Vietnamese. The decor was Chinese. There was no Disco to it, it was Korean Style Karaoke, so it was all private party rooms. The food offered was authentically Italian, if authentic Italian was pizza, churros and the like. It was not "Mega Awesome," it couldn't be, because it was Karaoke. So, the only accurate thing in the name was there was in fact Karaoke "performed" there, or "butchered," if one wanted to be more accurate. Nothing about the place was either Vietnamese or Japanese, both of which might have made sense given the name or activity.

Gretchen clung to my arm with the gusto that Joy somehow managed to cling to Jammer's despite the obvious height difference. We walked to the door and Jammer held it for everyone to enter.

We stood in the waiting gallery and an old Pilipino lady stood behind the register.

"Mister Mike, how are you?" she asked in flawless English. I know it's probably racist but seeing as she was an old Filipino lady I expected her to sound more Asian as opposed to bland Midwestern.

"I'm well, Ms. Hernandez. How are you?" Jammer smiled as the door shut with a chime behind us.

"We are all well. The usual room?" Ms. Hernandez asked. That was another thing, I knew Mr. Hernandez was Filipino too so the name didn't make sense, either. I knew that part of the Spanish American War was fought in the Philippines, but still, even if it'd been a Spanish colony... Hernandez?

Ms. Hernandez shuffled from behind the counter and moved down a hall opening Karaoke Gallery #3. Jammer took Joy's hand and lead her down the hall followed by Gretchen and I. Gretchen clung to my arm, and even for a guy like me who is as far removed from touchy-feely as porn is from Shakespeare, I found it damned appealing.

We entered Gallery #3 and the first thing I noticed was its red plush couches and small stage with red shag carpet complimented with gold fringe along the corners. There was a disco ball hanging annoyingly from the ceiling. The most modern thing in this 70's porno throwback room was the iPad on the table, which could be used to make a kitchen order where Mr. Hernandez worked. It also controlled the song selection.

This wasn't Jammer's first visit here. He liked doing business in Gallery #3. It was an interior room with no windows and sound-proofed. It was like it was custom built for drug dealing, or in Jammer's case, distributing.

"Thank you, Ms. Hernandez." Jammer beamed as he looked around the room like it was his favorite place on the planet. On one wall hung a poorly made painting of Elvis, on the other a painting of George Harrison.

I huffed.

"What?" Gretchen whispered.

I looked down to her and shrugged. I leaned close, her hair smelled kind of sweet and fruity, but I couldn't make out which, whispering, "I'm a Clapton man."

Gretchen laughed. "You heard about their guitar duel?'

"Hell yes!" Everyone worth a damn had to know about the Clapton Harrison guitar duel.

Ms. Hernandez left us, and Jammer picked up the iPad. "Who is going first at Asian Karaoke?"

"Jammer..." I tried to not sound annoyed but then again, I've tried a lot of things and screwed them up. "You don't have to say Asian Karaoke; all fuckin Karaoke is goddamned Asian."

"I don't think that's even remotely true." Jammer shook his head as he thumbed through the song list.

"No," Gretchen offered diplomatically, "I think Nick is right on this one."

"Well, " Jammer reasoned diplomatically, "we'll either agree to disagree or we chalk it up to being right twice a day."

"I'm not a broken goddamn watch, man."

"I dunno, you don't think Karaoke is Asian."

I sighed. "Jammer, obviously it's Asian but that doesn't mean it's Asian Karaoke. Karaoke was... you know what, I'm not fuckin doing this." I plopped down on one of the couches. Gretchen sat beside me and made sure my arm went around her shoulder.

Joy with an E-Y went first and belted out the Bangles *Heaven is a Place on Earth*. She had a set of pipes on her. As she sang, Gretchen whispered to me that Joy was going to be a contestant on one of those damned reality TV shows, but she'd gotten sick the day of the audition.

"What, made her not be able to sing?" I asked as Joy hit the chorus.

"Montezuma's revenge," Gretchen answered.

I let that line of the conversation drop at that point. I lacked the will and want to know more.

We all clapped as Joy took her bow at the end of her song.

"Who is going to be next?" Jammer asked.

Gretchen and I hollered simultaneously, "*You!*" I added an "asshole" to that, but the effect still stuck.

After the Army, I knew Jammer had worked as the player at a piano bar. His singing isn't bad, but obviously he got that job from his playing. He chose to "preform" the Cure's *Just Like Heaven*. Gretchen watched, Joy was held in rapt attention, and I looked through the food menu on the iPad.

Gretchen clapped at the end and Joy gave a standing ovation jumping up and down, which was impressive in those heels. We ordered some nachos, fried mozzarella sticks, chicken fingers, and Tacitos for Jammer.

"Okay," Jammer laughed, "who's gonna be next? Nick or Gretchen?"

"She is," I blurted as I touched my finger to my nose.

"Bastard," she gasped.

"Do you always throw girls under the bus?" Joy asked with a chuckle.

"You really don't know Nick Decker do you?" Jammer laughed and pulled the Greg Brady to get his arm around Joy's shoulders. He was never the smoothest guy, but he surprisingly pulled that off.

Joy leaned in and playfully pushed her forehead to his. "I don't know any of you, but Gretch silly."

Jammer smiled and must have gone cross-eyed being that close. "Nick's idea of chivalry isn't the most, how do you say, traditional?"

They laughed at my expense, but I didn't mind. I felt Gretchen reach up and squeeze my hand. Then she let go and took the iPad, flipping through the selection before mounting the stage. Jammer and Joy came over and plopped on the couch with me as the music began.

I couldn't take my eyes away as she began singing. I wasn't even paying attention to the words as much as I was just caught in the feel.

She got to the chorus, *Motorin' what's your price for flight? And finding Mister Right? We'll be alright tonight.*"

Jammer leaned over. "Bro, she's got a beautiful Mezzo-Soprano."

"All of her is fuckin hot," I retorted in a whisper.

"No dumbass," he hissed, "Mezzo-Soprano is a voice type. She's got a gorgeous voice."

"I knew that."

"Bullshit." He laughed then leaned back against Joy's side.

Some people preform, but Gretchen genuinely seemed to have fun up there. She danced and moved with the mic stand as she performed Night Ranger's song.

When she finished, I clapped with the rest. I clapped non-sarcastically, possibly for the first time in my life with the exception of the Flogging Molly concert where I finally got to hear *It's Been The Worst Day Since Yesterday* played live and when David Tennant preformed as Hamlet in *Hamlet.* That second one wasn't live but on a Blu-ray, but I thought his performance warranted the ovation, so damn it he got it.

She hopped off stage and stuck the landing, heels be damned. I stood up and she flung herself in my arms. I spun her around. It felt right, and that was weird. I set her down and she licked her lower lip. "Your turn."

Goddammit.

I sighed. "Can I skip and just be a spectator?"

"ASIAN KARAOKE!" Jammer yelled with a laugh.

"Asian Karaoke," Joy agreed.

Gretchen reached up and brushed the back of her fingertips along my jaw. "Asian Karaoke, Nick."

I grabbed the iPad, scrolled to the best band in the world, picked one of their top three songs and got on the stage grabbing the mic. I can't sing. As in, at all.

The guitar riff tore through the speakers and instead of Bon Scott, my audience of three got me belting out *Highway to Hell.*

I probably looked as ridiculous as I sounded. I felt like I should be arrested for what I was doing to such a classic piece of art.

Gretchen smiled as she watched, and I could see her sing along as I got to the chorus.

Gretchen and Joy both got up to dance at the beginning of the second verse. Which I butchered. It was obviously which of the two was the stripper and other the waitress. Maybe heel size had something to do with it? I doubted it, though.

At the end of the song I put the mic back on the stand because let's be honest, my singing would never be worthy of a mic drop. Plus with my luck, I'd drop and break it and have to pay for it.

I stepped off stage and Gretchen clapped. She leaned into my side as I sat next to her and whispered, "You looked like a preteen juxtaposition at a pedophile grammar teacher convention."

"The fuck?" I asked, because honestly, how the hell do you reply to that?

There was a knock at the door and Jammer opened it to let Mr. Hernandez come in with the tray of food and drinks which she set on the table. I hadn't ordered a drink, but there was a Dr. Pepper there for me. With the main active ingredient in Dr. Pepper being prune juice it was probably the healthiest thing in my diet.

We sat and ate, and then Joy suggested "Duets."

"No," I said.

Jammer laughed at how quick I answered.

"You know what that means?" Joy said with a laugh at Jammer. Gretchen, answered for him.

"That means Jammer and Nick go first!"

They laughed and clapped. Jammer pulled me protesting to my feet and started through the iPad selection.

"No...no... fuck no... no... no..." I said, as he would point to different songs. "Are you Kenny or Dolly?" I asked as he stopped.

"Kenny," he said adamantly.

"No." I shook my head.

"Okay, Dolly." He sounded excited at the compromise.

"Still no..." I shot that down faster than if it were a Sopwith with Manfred von Richthofen behind it in a Fokker DR1.

Finally, we picked one and got on stage.

"Are there two mics'?" I asked.

"No," Jammer answered as the music started. What we settled on, much to the amusement of the girls, was David Bowie's *Space Oddity*. Jammer was Ground Control, and I was Major Tom. The girls playfully helped with the countdown.

The girls clapped as we finished and took far less time to pick a duet for themselves. Jammer and I sat as they began, though I'd argue their song wasn't as much a duet as it was a song sung simultaneously. But who could bitch about watching Gretchen and Joy with an E-Y have fun dancing together singing The Runaway's *Cherry Bomb*? On the chorus, Gretchen would point to me when they sang "Hello, Daddy," and to Jammer with "Hello, Mom." I don't know what her desired effect was, but there was an effect.

They finished, and we clapped, then Jammer called out with a mouthful of Tacito, "Gretchen! Sing a song about Nick!"

Gretchen laughed and flipped through the iPad.

She danced as she sang. It was a sexy, rising and falling undulating thing that reminded me of something the singer in a 1920's speakeasy would do as she performed for a crowd enjoying their imported alcohol, which was an order of magnitude better in quality to the bath tub gin places who couldn't afford a singer like her could afford. The way that dress hugged her didn't help the illusion.

She started to sing 'Favorite' by Liz Phair and when she got to the chorus she pointed to me. Again, I don't know what effect she was going for, but there was an effect.

When she finished, she got a standing ovation, and I got a hug, and I'm pretty sure she realized the effect she had on me. A boy can dream, even daydream, right?

Jammer and Joy got up and sang Elton John and KeeKee Dee's *Don't Go Breaking My Heart.* Then Gretchen and I demanded she sing a song about Jammer.

She chose Heart's *All I Wanna Do Is Make Love to You.* I knew I had to at least give Jammer a heads up on the whole "E-Y" thing. I'm not saying he shouldn't go for it, but if you're gonna cliff dive you deserve to know about possible rocks.

They then demanded that Gretchen duet. We flipped through the iPad. Gretchen turned her back to Joy and Jammer. "We'll pick one that I do the heavy lifting." I smiled gratefully. She chose Faith Hill's *Just to Hear You Say That You Love Me.* The Tim McGraw part was by far the easier and way fewer words.

After we fell together on the couch, we ate a bit and relaxed.

"Jammer?" I asked.

"Yeah, buddy?"

"Not that this isn't fun," I really didn't want to sing any more, or at all, if I were to be completely honest. "When does Peaches get here?"

Jammer looked bashful. “Oh, we’re meeting him for lunch tomorrow.”

Gretchen’s eyes narrowed. “You said you needed a date for the meet.”

“Yeah…”. He looked guilty. “I didn’t have anything to do tonight.”

I sighed. The only thing worse than Karaoke was being tricked into Asian Karaoke. “Goddammit.”

XI: Butch and Sundance or Bonnie and Clyde

The girls were on stage singing Cindy Lauper's version of *Time After Time.* I say the Cindy Lauper version because I can't remember if she did the original or a remake, but remakes have definitely been done. Jammer and I sat on one of the sofa's. I was digging into a Fried Mozzarella stick and he was attacking a Tacito like it was Omaha beach and he was the Tom Hanks in *Saving Private Ryan*.

I leaned over before the girls got to the first chorus. "Jammer."

He looked to me around a mouthful of Tacito. "Yeah, buddy."

"I dunno if there's a protocol for this, but yeah. Joy's a post-op tranny, bro."

Jammer looked confused. "A post-op tranny bro?"

I shook my head. "No, she's a post-op tranny. The *bro* was addressed to you."

He sighed and took a sip of his drink. "Oh, whew, I mean they are tacking so many damned letters LGBTUVWXYZ acronym I just figured 'post-op tranny bro' was something new I hadn't heard of yet." He did sound relieved.

"Yeah, sorry I made that confusing." I couldn't decide if Jammer had a point or if he were an asshole. Yes? No? Both? It was probably a safe bet the answer was both.

Jammer laughed. "I think society's insistence on labels is what makes it confusing. Why can't people just be people?"

"Fair enough." I couldn't help but smirk; Jammer had always been the kind of guy who can draw those out of you.

He reached over and clapped my good knee. "But yeah, I know. Thanks for the heads up though, good looking out."

"You already knew?" There was suspicion in my voice. Joy was a subtle girl, not the crazy plastic look that makes you think of a hooker that easily can be a stereotype.

Jammer shot me an incredulous look. "I'm a fucking medic, bro."

"And a goddamned great one at that." I clinked my plastic cup to his and sipped my Dr. Pepper.

"I know a little Adam's apple is still an Adam's apple, you fucker." He chuckled and sipped his drink to the toast.

"So, everything's groovy?" I asked as the girls shared the mic and hit the last chorus. "Don't need me to make up a polite exit for you?"

Jammer watching the stage. "No, we're cool." He smiled. "I ever tell you the hottest chick I've ever seen was a dude in Thailand?"

"On multiple fuckin occasions." It was one of his most oft quoted sayings.

Jammer smiled and winked at me, it was a wink that seemed to involve his entire damned face. It was a wink that was the opposite of subtle. If subtle were a victim, Jammer's wink was its brutal rapist.

We clapped as the girl's finished. There was a knock on the door and when Jammer opened it Ms. Hernandez stepped inside.

"Mister Mike." Though she spoke in perfect English, the way she said Mister came out *Meesta*. It reminded me of the kids in Iraq who would come up to you "*Meesta Meesta*, chicken, five-dollar." Then you'd give them five bucks, they'd come back with a cooked chicken and five pieces of good Iraqi flatbread. You knew at five dollars they were ripping you off, but it wasn't a meal rejected by Ethiopians or served out of a goddamned marmite.

Now every time I see kids standing outside a liquor store playing the Mister Mister game, in my head it always sounds *Meesta Meesta*.

Ms. Hernandez held out an iPad-mini and Jammer took it, giving it an intense study. He waved me over. I came and we were looking at security feed from the front of Little Saigon Mega Awesome Disco Karaoke. Parked out in the lot were ten Heaven's Hotdogs straddling their Yamaha cruisers.

"Ms. Hernandez," Jammer said, his voice manic yet authoritative. "I need you to kill the security feed and erase the files of us showing up and being here."

"Then," I jumped in, "you and Mr. Hernandez need to get in the kitchen and behind the fridge, or a counter. Anything that's heavy and made of steel. Got it?"

She nodded with understanding. She knew what Jammer did. Deep down that sweet lady was as libertarian capitalist as Jammer and I were. "I'll message the room's iPad when we're ready."

Jammer gave her a hug and kissed her forehead before she left. The door closed behind her and Jammer nodded. "Okay, Gretchen, you and Joy are going out the back way. Nick and I will distract the shitheads out front as you two get clear." He was nodding confidently as he looked to me. "Butch Cassidy and the Sundance Kid time."

"Which of you is who?" Gretchen asked.

"Butch," Jammer said, answering at the same time as me. Jammer added effect to this by pointing to himself. To be fair, I pointed to him as well. Then I pointed to myself and Jammer pointed to me, oddly accusatorily as we both said, "Sundance."

Gretchen chewed her lip in thought while Joy with an E-Y was shaking. Gretchen walked over and slid her arm around her friend. It was an odd sight; her friend Joy dwarfed Gretchen but there was no doubt which of them was the rock. Gretchen finally nodded in agreement. "I can see that, Butch and Sundance, but this isn't that movie."

"Huh?" Jammer asked.

Gretchen smiled, flashing her pearly whites. "This is Bonnie and Clyde."

I got what she was suggesting but it hadn't dawned on Jammer yet.

"Jammer," she continued, "you're going to get Joy out the back," I couldn't tell if there was an innuendo there. "Nick and I will deal with what's out front."

I noticed with both plans it was I being volunteered for the harder route, but that's life, I guess. In the army we called it being "voluntold." Sadly, even I had to admit it was the right call.

"You notice in all those movies," Joy added with a shaking voice, "the characters die right?"

Gretchen chewed her lip nervously. "Buffy and Spike?" She offered.

I shook my head, "This feels more western and I don't have a cool trench coat."

"Cort and the Blonde Stranger from *The Quick and the Dead?*" Gretchen suggested as she gave Joy a reassuring squeeze.

I chewed on it then suggested with inquisitively raised eyebrows. "Shirley McClane and Clint Eastwood, *Two Mules for Sister Sarah*?"

Gretchen smiled. "Ohhh, I like that."

I nodded and pulled out my OD Green coated Springfield 1911 and spun it in my hand and held it over to Jammer, grip first. He looked at it curiously, so I shrugged. "Can't protect the girl with your dick in your hand."

He laughed and reached behind his back under the tweed jacket and came out with a shiny nickel-plated Kimber 1911. "How about you keep your green shit in your own dick-beater. If you're seriously going out the front with the stripper, you're going to need it."

"Hey!" Gretchen said, scowling, then added curiously, "Why do you both carry .45's?"

"We're old school," I offered.

"Nick and I both have little bitch hands," Jammer said with sickening pride, "so it's easier to get meat around a single stack mag for better control than it is around a double-stack 9mm and .40 cal grips."

I sighed. "Jesus Christ, Jammer..."

"That's silly," Gretchen said. "Even a Glock 17 or 19 isn't that unwieldy. You two could have the larger ammo capacity if you were carrying something more modern."

"Well, are you carrying?" Jammer retorted.

"Yes," she said sheepishly. "I got eight Ninja shuriken throwing stars, and two ASP's."

Jammer's jaw dropped. "Where?"

She pulled them out of her leather half jacket. The ASP's, which are small collapsible hardened steel batons popped out of the sleeves.

"No gun?" I asked, hoping she was going to smile and pull an MP-5 from somewhere inventive and disturbing. No such luck.

She shook her head. "My pistols are at Jammer's."

Jammer kicked his left foot up on the table knocking over drinks and the nachos. He hiked up his pants leg and pulled off an ankle holster with bearing a snub-nosed, nickel-plated .357 and one half-moon speed loader.

"Here," he said handing it over to Gretchen. "It's better than nothing."

"Jammer why the hell is all your shit nickel-plated?" I asked with a disapproving tone in my voice. I just couldn't hide it. I still thought of Jammer and myself as soldiers, or at least professionals. Professionals don't carry shit like that.

He shrugged. "I'm an illicit substance distributor." Jammer had a nice way of prettying up the reality of *I make and distribute drugs to drug dealers*.

I smiled. "You always were a drama queen."

"And you never learned to play your part." His smile seemed melancholy.

I felt Gretchen move over to my side as I asked Jammer, "Want to clue me into what it is?"

"In Fallujah—"

"Don't," I interrupted.

"In Afghanistan you—"

"Jammer… no." My rebuke was soft, but it landed, and he gave up.

"Yea. You know what the fuck you are, Nick Decker." His voice was adamant. He opened his arms and pulled me into a hug. It was a man hug, the warrior embrace. Three pats on the back with your non-weapon hand and then break. We clasped our hands to the other's forearm and squeezed.

"Strength and Honor, brother." It was tradition, so I said it, but that doesn't mean I didn't mean it. We shook, and then I looked to Gretchen. She looked oddly moved.

"Gretchen," Jammer sounded nonchalant, very Jammer-esque. "You take care of our boy, all right?"

Gretchen smiled and wrapped her arms around Jammer. He was two inches shorter than me, but his chin still fit on top of her head.

Jammer whispered, "He's the best friend I got." I knew I wasn't supposed to hear, it but I did. Gretchen smiled and leaned up and kissed Jammer's bearded cheek.

I stepped over to Joy with an E-Y and shook her hand. "Good meeting you, Joy." I smiled but my voice went cold and business-like. "You move when he says move, you duck when he says duck, you do exactly what Jammer tells you to do, got it? He'll get you through this."

Joy was nervous. Jammer was a drug distributor. I was a private investigator. Gretchen was apparently a member of some shadowy secret society. Joy with an E-Y was a post-op transsexual stuck in a really shitty situation. So nervous made sense. But she nodded with a metallic – though fake– determination.

The iPad dinged and Jammer checked it. He set it down and looked up to me. "They're ready."

I felt a smirk tug at the corner of my lips. I opened the door and held it for the ladies. Jammer came out last. I let the door close before Gretchen and I turned to the right while Jammer and Joy turned to the left.

The pistol felt comfortable in my hand. I was too comfortable in situations like this to ever be what I'd consider a good man… Jammer either. We weren't good men, but in situations that turned shitty fast, we were necessary men. Maybe that's why we were friends? Or was it because deep down, we were kindred assholes.

I looked at my friend who smiled. It was fake but heartfelt. He was playing the part that was needed. Yet there was no hiding the fact that he'd rather be going out the front door with me guns a blazing. Everyone dies, right? Is there a better way than to go than with guns raging, backing up your friend? Well, besides Horatius at the Bridge? Horatius at the Bridge always wins.

The girls both stopped as they noticed Jammer and I not moving. But we both knew it was time to go.

I smirked, "Smoke me a kipper, I'll be back for breakfast." Playing my part as much as he was.

Jammer's head bobbed, and he grinned like a school kid who just got the prom queen's phone number while her quarterback boyfriend was away in the bathroom. "See you, Space Cowboy."

We turned and neither looked back.

Gretchen and I walked side by side down the garish hallway. I heard her breach and check to make sure there were six .357 rounds in the cylinder before snapping it shut.

"Hold this," she said and stuffed the revolver in my left hand.

I watched as she pulled out one of her shuriken and use the razor like cutting edge to cut the dress so that it ended above mid-thigh as the rest of the fabric fell to her ankles. She kept the shuriken in her left hand as she kicked off her heels, then smiled as she held out her hand for the weapon. I handed it to her and then we simultaneously, like we'd planned it that way, thumbed back the hammers of our pistols.

We smiled; it was time to go to work.

XII: Shadows of the Night

The good news was the windows of the establishment were tinted to the point they couldn't see in from the parking lot, but we could see them. They all sat in the parking lot straddling their bikes. I was pretty sure they didn't know we were there. However, they might be expecting us to show.

"Do we have a plan?" Gretchen asked quietly.

"If they see us, I'm fairly fucking sure their plan is another car chase. I don't think they know we're here. I think they're just watching this place because they know Jammer comes here for business and I'd likely go to Jammer for help."

Gretchen nodded. "That makes sense. So, what's the plan?"

"We're going to walk out and kill'em right there in the damned parking lot."

She looked over to me, not in horror of the suggestion of murder but the simplicity of it.

"What?" I shrugged.

"I just kinda expected more, is all." She smiled, so that was something.

"They're expecting a fight out there on the road. Look at 'em, they're still on their bikes. So, we don't give them what they want. They want the fight out there? We give it to 'em right freaking here."

Gretchen nodded in agreement. "We hit them, fall back, and use the cars for cover, If pushed we fall back to here."

"Fuckin' A." I've never really had a girl get me. It felt nice. Soul Mate stuff, I guess.

Gretchen walked behind the counter and looked under it before laughing.

"What?" I asked, not taking my eyes from the Heaven's Hotdogs.

"I expected to find a shotgun under here."

"No joy?" I asked with a smile.

"Not in regard to firepower, no." She milled about for a moment. "Apparently there are outside speakers I can set on a timer."

I smirked. "Any good music?"

"I'll come up with something." She sounded very assured. She played around for a moment then came back to my side. I tore my eyes from the bikers and looked to her.

"Why are you doing this?"

She looked up to me. "I don't really know, but I did know I'd hate myself if you came out here and I wasn't with you."

I looked at her a moment. "If we were sixteen and in high school, I'd ask you to be my girlfriend."

She looked back at me incredulously. "When you were sixteen I was one." She smiled and said jokingly, "Freaking pervert."

"Forget I said it." I looked back to the bikers.

"Nope, I can't," she laughed. "You said it, now it's out there in the universe never to be taken back."

I chuckled. "You're kind of a bitch."

She giggled. "And you're kind of a bastard, Nick."

We moved to the door. Just before I could push it open, she asked, "Any inspiring words?"

I chewed the inside of my cheek for a moment. "Ever read the *Iliad*?"

She nodded.

"*Sarpedon*," I suggested.

Now she shook her head. "Remind me."

"Lets get glory or give it to those cockbags, or something like that."

She held the shuriken in her left hand and the .357 in the right. "Works for me."

I pushed open the door with my back. Gretchen stepped out and I rolled off so it could close behind us then we stepped calmly out into the parking lot. There were five cars and at least seventy yards between Gretchen and I, and the spot where the bikers were huddled on their bikes under a light in the parking lot. Pistols at this range were basically useless. Mandy Bachman and Rob Leatham probably could have made the shots. But I was willing to bet Gretchen was not Mandy Bachman and I knew for a fact I'm not Rob Leatham.

Gretchen definitely played the part. She laughed and leaned into my side, hiding her pistol behind my back. If I didn't know her or the plan, I'd assumed she was the girl who had had fun on her karaoke date, that's how good Gretchen was.

I made sure my .45 was hidden behind my thigh. I leaned in and kissed the top of her head. Her hair still smelled nice. She laughed annoyingly loud which caused some of the bikers to look over then immediately look away. No one likes people that cloyingly in love. She was managing to hide us in plain sight and doing it with the skill of the world's most talented illusionist.

There was twenty yards and two cars between us and the bikers. The first was a Ford F-150 and the second and closest to the bikers was a banged up 1975 golden-brown Chevy Nova. We eased our way past the F-150 on the side away from the bikers and began moving to the Nova like it was our car. This was the first time we took serious notice from the bikers.

Some people would look at the collection of ten Heaven's Hotdogs and think, *oh no bikers*. My thought was, a sawed-off double-barrel 12 gauge, an MP-10 (like an MP-5 sub machine gun but firing 10mm rounds instead of 9mm), a nice Franchi SPAS 12-gauge pump, 2 Uzi's, and five guys with assorted pistols. Some people would look at that assortment and think, we're fucked. I looked at that assortment and though, we're *probably* fucked. There is a big difference between those two.

Two things happened simultaneously; several bikers noticed us and gave us real attention, and the music started.

The speakers blared the voice of Pat Benatar, singing *Shadow of the Night*. And like that, for a moment, every biker except one of the guys with an UZI looked away from us and back to the front door of Little Saigon Mega Awesome Disco Karaoke.

Without a word we started running, Gretchen around the front of the Nova and me behind the back. The biker closest to me was one of the guys with an Uzi but it was in his right hand and his left side was facing me. He jerked his head from the door and his eyes went wide as he saw me raising my pistol. He started turning to face me and tried to get his arm around while still straddling the bike.

He had blue eyes.

I aimed at his left shoulder, knowing I was going to jerk the trigger. The pistol barked in my hand. The round caught him in the center of his chest just where the zipper of his vest ended. It seemed a relatively small hole in the front, but the hollow point opened up inside him, blowing a huge hole out his back. His arms flailed and he went over, taking the Yamaha with him in a clatter.

All that happened in less than a second. I now had both hands on the pistol and aimed at the next closest biker. He was trying to get his pistol aimed around to me. With a good two-handed grip, I aimed square at his head. He was five yards away. I pressed the trigger and the back of the man's head exploded. I shifted aim to the third biker positioned between the two I'd already shot but further back, about ten yards, armed with that nice Franchi-SPAS 12. I cooked off two shots, the first hitting just high and right of the heart, the second just low and to the left of it. His heart was intact, but he was dead whether he noticed it or not.

I noticed other things in this time, like what Gretchen was doing. As I fired my first round she threw her shuriken. At first I thought it missed the biker who was not the closest to her, but one about five yards away armed with the other Uzi, but then I saw the spurt of arterial blood gush from his neck. He dropped the Uzi and grabbed at his newfound geyser. As I was getting my headshot, Gretchen grabbed the right wrist of the biker holding the double-barreled sawed off. She literally pushed the .357 to his forehead and pulled the trigger. With her left hand she tore the sawed-off from the dead man's grasp. She then jumped backwards landing on the hood of the Nova. She aimed between her raised knees and shot two rounds into the chest of a biker with a ridiculously large revolver and a bike chain... not a motorcycle chain, but a kids BMX bike chain.

As Gretchen somersaulted backwards off the Nova hood to take cover behind the car, I started moving back around behind the trunk to join her on the driver's side. I found the guy with the MP-10 and the first round I shot at him punched into the Yamaha's gas tank. In the movies they explode, and that would have come in handy, but in reality had it been a movie explosion, Gretchen and I would've died too. However, in a movie we'd just have some attractive scratches.

My second shot at him punched into his hip. At the very least it probably broke it and if he was on his feet he'd have fallen, but with the bike under him he was still up. He started shooting in an uncontrolled burst that shattered the rear window of the Nova and started pinging across the trunk. My third shot punched under his raised left arm that was supporting the MP-10 and slammed into his sternum slightly above his left floating rib. His whole body shuttered, his arms flailed, and the MP-10 fell from his hand and flopped around on its sling.

I gave him one more .45 ACP center mass to finish the job. Overkill can indeed be under fucking rated. The slide of my 1911 locked to the rear and I thumbed the mag release as I spun around the edge of the car, ducking down behind the tire. I jerked a fresh magazine from under my right arm and rammed it into the pistol's grip. I dropped the slide and looked to Gretchen who was standing behind the driver's door. She angled up leaning her arms on the hood cooking off three shots, taking down if not outright killing one of the bikers running for the fallen Uzi. She then crouched behind the driver's door and opened the revolver's cylinder and punched out the spent casings.

I ran crouched over to her and pushed her over till she was sitting crouched behind the tire. She looked at me confused and angry as she grabbed the speed-loader. I popped up high enough to see. I shot through the windshield and passenger window of the Nova, catching one of the bikers in the hip and causing him to half spin and fall screaming. I moved back down the car toward the rear wheel. I felt the Nova's rear passenger window explode as three 9mm rounds punched through it thrown from a Glock 19. I fired twice but the biker was hidden behind his bike. More 9mm rounds punched the body of the Nova as I got behind the wheel.

I didn't count the rounds, but I did hear the biker yell: "Heaven's above!" I came around the car at a sprint and jumped high and planted both feet on the stand side of the bike, giving it all my momentum. I landed on my back with a painful thud as the bike fell over on the biker who cried out in a mixture of pain and impotent rage. I wasted no time, I didn't even get to my feet, I just scrambled over the bike, pressed the pistol where the jaw met the back of the man's ear, angled it away from me, and ducked as I pulled the trigger. The bike blocked most of the back splash but the sleeve of the white shirt I borrowed from Jammer could have used some bleach.

I pulled myself to my feet and started looking around, making sure each man was dead or at least out of the fight. The man who had taken the shuriken to the neck was out of the fight; a .45 ACP made him dead. I then looked to Gretchen.

"Go hot wire Jammer's car."

She nodded, holding the .357 and the sawed off double barrel and turned to sprint to Jammer's Accord.

I recovered my spent magazine and stuffed it in the empty slot in my underarm rig. I then holstered my .45 as I picked up the MP-10. I found five more magazines in the guy's saddlebag. The MP-10 had a Tac-Light on it. Had he hit me with the 500 Lumens of that, I'd be dead because he could have taken his time. I flicked the switch and realized the Tac-Light had no batteries. I slung it over my shoulder and then grabbed the Franchi-SPAS with its sling holding ten more shells. The shells looked odd, and I realized it wasn't loaded with Buck, but with Dragon's Breath rounds, which are basically phosphorus flamethrower rounds. These assholes hadn't been playing around.

I did notice all these guys had the same tattoo on their chest. It appeared to be a phrase but not in English. I snapped a quick pic of one and stuffed my phone back in my pocket.

I picked up a half-spent HK P-30 and two extra mags for it along with one of the Uzi's and three mags sticking out of the dead man's belt. I grabbed a leather backpack from where it was strapped to one of the bikes and stuffed it with the weapons and ammo. Tires screeched as Gretchen pulled the Accord to a stop. I moved to the passenger's side and tossed the bag into the floorboard, then the shotgun, and held the MP-10 as I climbed inside. Gretchen was pulling away as I was shutting the door.

The entire gunfight took less than twenty seconds. Hot-wiring the car and gathering the guns had taken around a minute. In the background, I could still hear the chorus of *Shadows of the Night* as it blared in the background.

I knew I'd have to add it to the Gunfight Mix.

XIII: Saul's Pistol and Pawn

There was no traffic as Gretchen deftly navigated the after-midnight streets. We could see clubs with cars, people and traffic, but Gretchen avoided them.

"Do we have a plan?" she asked.

We were both still keyed up, adrenaline pumping. "Know where Saul's Pistol and Pawn is?"

She shook her head, then added, "No," in case I wasn't paying attention.

"It's on the corner of Decatur and 75th." I looked over to her and up and down her form in the newly shortened dress. "You okay? Hurt anywhere?"

She shook her head again.

"No, you're not okay or no you're not hurt anywhere?" I reached over and grabbed the wheel with my left hand. "Take both hands and feel everywhere. Make sure there isn't anything fucked up you haven't noticed yet."

I kept my eyes on the road as she checked, even though I would have loved to pay more attention to her thighs.

She put her hands back on the wheel. "Just an abrasion on my knee." She glanced at me. "By the way, why did you push me back there?"

"There's no cover under the car." I dropped my partially spent mag from my .45 and popped the round from the chamber before loading my last fresh magazine. I dropped the slide and lowered the hammer before putting the round back in the partially spent mag. Everything went back to their home in the holster rig under my jacket.

"Hell, even with the metal of an old Nova, it's easy to punch through a car. So safest place is behind the engine block or a wheel well, because the steel in the rims and axel will protect you." I looked over to her. "Had they been smart enough to know to lay down, they could have shot you from under the car, which would've finished you like that." I snapped my fingers to emphasize my point.

She chewed her lower lip for a moment as she calculated everything in her mind, playing the "what if, what could have happened" game.

"Thanks Nick."

"Don't mention it."

"I've never been in a gun fight before." She sounded apologetic.

"Well, you handled yourself like a pro." I took the double-barreled shotgun she'd acquired and opened the breach, finding two double OO buck shells from the newly acquired bag, reloaded and shut it.

"Thanks." She turned onto Decatur Street and stopped as the next light turned red. She looked over to me. "You can train for stuff you know..."

I reached over and squeezed her hand even as she held the wheel. "You are the only broad I've ever said this to, but I'd go into the shit with you any day, Gretchen."

She smiled, and the car behind us honked as the light turned green. "My people will be after us by now as well, Nick."

"Oh yeah?" I sounded nonchalant, but let's be honest, all I needed was more shit on the pile.

"I've missed three check-ins." She looked grave.

I chuckled. "They sound like annoying parents."

She smiled, lightening the gravity that seemed to have been pulling at her soul. "If you don't trust me I'll go, if it's going to make you feel safer."

"Why *are* you with me?" I took my eyes off the road long enough to look at her profile in the passing headlights.

She glanced over. "If they wanted you for a good reason they'd have brought you in with a team. They don't send a Sister in Shadow after someone they want positive things for."

"Why are you with me?" I repeated calmly, curiously.

"I don't want them to get you." She looked to me and started to reach over, then stopped herself.

"Why?" I reached over and took her hand again. This time she took it off the wheel and interlaced her fingers with mine.

"Just something about you. Even when I was just studying the files." She went silent for a few blocks. "If you want me to go, I will."

How do you tell someone, *Our shared Guardian Angel Bruce Campbell told me you and I are soulmates.* I squeezed her hand and it felt good in mine.

She looked over to me and smiled.

Saul's Pistol and Pawn was not owned by a guy born with the name Saul. Saul had been born Yuri Ivan Preobrazhensky in Leningrad in 1960. He'd joined the Russian army and become a Paratrooper in 1978. He'd been in on the initial invasion of Afghanistan in the 80's. There, he'd decided he wasn't a fan of the communist system. Yuri loaded up a pack and pulled a Berghdal, but without being an asshole about it. He'd evaded his own people and the mujahedeen, crossed the border into Pakistan, and wandered up to the U.S. Marine Guard at the U.S. Consulate in Peshawar. Then in broken English, with a *Draganov* and a smile, said, "'Allo, I Yuri Ivan Preobrazhensky am seek poly-icle ass-eye-la-em."

He ended up coming to the U.S., taking an ESL class, and then joined the Army again, this time the American one. He ended up fighting in Grenada and Panama before getting out. His big accomplishment he'd made in the American Military though, was with his ability at cards. In his time in the Army, he'd made and saved away about fifty-thousand dollars playing cards. With that money, he'd come and bought out Saul's Pistol and Pawn from old man Saul Utivitz, a holocaust survivor who was looking to retire and move to Israel where his brother lived in the settlements. Not to confuse anyone and to feel more American, also so he wouldn't have to buy new signs, Yuri changed his legal name to Saul.

Yuri was one of those fellows who lived on a neat grey line; not in the black or the white. He wouldn't deal in stolen goods. And if something slipped in, he actually did his best to get it to the original owner even at a cost to himself, but he kept his ear to the ground. He wouldn't deal in stolen, but he'd point someone the way to someone who would. He wouldn't sell guns to someone he shouldn't, but he'd tell someone who shouldn't where they could acquire what they were looking for. Saul was clean, but he knew the dirt, and he turned a blind eye to shady.

We parked behind the dumpster in the ally and covered the weapons we'd taken in the back seat. We made our way around to the front of the shop and pulled open the door to the ringing of a bell. Saul–Yuri worked the shop at night because his wife Mary-Jo was a night nurse at the hospital in the pediatric ward. This kept them on the same schedule. I saw him sitting at the counter, facing the door. I also knew he had a Makarov pistol under the counter pointed at me and Gretchen.

I held my right hand out, fingers spread and waved with my left. "Hey, Tovarishch." His hair was grey and wild. His strong features in his youth had sagged into near bulldog like jowls. The once fit paratrooper of two armies was now portly.

"Ah," he said and smiled, recognizing me. "My friend Nicolai." He was missing several teeth from adventures in his earlier life. I watched as Yuri lifted his hand from under the counter and sat the Makarov pistol on the counter in plain sight. In all honesty, I couldn't think of a finer compliment Yuri gave anyone. "Nicolai, you have friend today?" He glanced up and down Gretchen's lithe form. "Nicolai, you friend have no shoes."

I held the door and Gretchen slid past. She smiled amiably. "He does have a friend today. With no shoes."

Yuri smiled. "I say this many many times. I say Nicolai, if Yuri can find good woman who have job and great cook, and be-u-t-ful, then handsome young man who work hard like he do," he pointed to me. "He very hard, diligent working man. You, young lady, could do much much worse. But where shoes?"

I never understood how Yuri could stumble over "beautiful" but nail "diligent."

Gretchen smiled. "Well, we've not known each other long." She glanced over to me and somehow that smile grew. "But we've just seemed to click. But I have no shoes because he swept me off my feet."

Yuri smiled and clapped a hand to his gut. "Nicolai, this is be-u-t-ful woman. I, Yuri, approve very very much!"

"Thanks, Yuri." I slid my arm around Gretchen's waist and squeezed her to my side. Yuri seemed pleased with the effect.

He smiled, but it slowly faded. "I take this is not visit to introduce Yuri to your pretty lady friend?" He pronounced "lady" with a *t*.

"Yeah, I'm afraid this is business." I stepped deeper into the shop. It was filled with the usual pawn shop clutter: a collection of not quite up-to-date TV's and stereos, various guitars hanging on the wall brought in by guys whose bands are going to make it but are in a jam right now, amps left by guys who needed rent money, and keyboards left by people whose dreams had gone the way of the dodo. There was also jewelry in cases which represented relationships that had shit in the bathtub, cameras and camcorders enough to shoot a found footage horror film, even some clothes and phones. It was the detritus of badly budgeted lives.

"I'm gonna need the back room."

Yuri's eyes narrowed. "You in trouble, Nicolai?"

"Nothing I can't handle," I said with a lackadaisical smirk. It's easier to lie to the people you care about. They already trust you and you can even lie to yourself and say it's for their benefit. Lying to yourself isn't the dangerous one; it's when you start believing them that you're screwed.

Yuri walked around the counter to the door and locked the gate, hanging a sign that read "#2, back in 10 minutes." He then walked to a heavy steel door and unlocked the padlock holding a crossbar in place, then the two padlocks on the door. He then stuck a key in the deadbolt and turned it, then stuck a different key in the handle and the door opened.

It was a long narrow room about twenty feet deep, ten feet wide. The back wall was full of shelves holding boxes and cases of ammo. There was a small counter holding various pistols of eclectic makes and models, and the back wall was covered in rifles and shotguns. Yuri moved behind the counter and placed his hands on it gravely. "What can Yuri do to help?"

I walked along the shelves and grabbed five boxes of 00 buck shot, then I grabbed four boxes of 10mm ammo. I also took two boxes of 9mm ammo and two boxes of .45ACP's. All this I stacked on the counter behind me as I watched Yuri's face grow grave with each additional box of rounds and shells. I sat down the last box and looked to him. "Do you have any more of those 8-round Wilson Combat 1911 Mags?"

He nodded and reached under the counter, coming up with five magazines. I reached back and added another box of .45ACP's to the stack.

"Nicolai," Yuri said slowly as he was writing everything up on a ticket. "I worry for you."

I was touched by the concern, "What's the damage my friend?"

He scribbled on the ticket then went to a calculator punching in numbers. I knew Yuri could do the math in his head, but he was stalling for time. That made me itchy and I glanced at the door. "Anything else?" Yuri asked as he wrote up the ticket.

"Some batteries for a Sure-Fire Tac-Light."

He reached under the counter and pullout out a small box of batteries made by Sure Fire.

"Dis," Yuri gestured at everything, "dis make us even. For what you did for Mary-Jo sister, da?"

I had gotten proof that Mary Jo's sister's husband had been beating her, and when they went to court, he arrived with his left leg in a cast and a knee that wasn't going to work quite right ever again. I shook my head. "Yuri this is too much for that man. How much do I owe you?"

He sat down the calculator and ticket pad, walked over to me and leaned across the counter very close. He had had borsch for dinner. "Dis make us even da?"

He walked back out into the store and came back with a craftsman tool bag and began loading the ammo inside. "Yuri not know what trouble you in," he glanced at Gretchen, "but if you want to leave your lady friend, she safe with Yuri and Mary-Jo."

You could tell Gretchen was touched by the way she smiled. "Thank you, Yuri." She walked over and placed her hands on the counter to lift her short frame to lean in and kiss Yuri's cheek. "Nick has the most amazing friends. It makes me jealous."

Yuri blushed. "You Nicolai's friend, you Yuri's friend."

I held out my hand and Yuri's engulfed it.

I walked out of Saul's Pistol and Pawn with a tool-bag containing a hundred shotgun shells, two hundred rounds of 10mm, a hundred rounds of 9mm, a hundred and fifty rounds of .45ACP's, and an empty green army duffle bag. Gretchen walked out wearing a new, used outfit and new, used shoes.

XIV: Awkward as F#*k

We ditched Jammer's car in a municipal parking deck. We took the ticket but never planned on paying it or picking the car up so neither of us checked the hourly or daily rates. I topped off my 1911 mags in the car as Gretchen drove, two under my right arm and the fresh one in the pistol. Before we got out of the car, I held over one of the HK P-30 9mm's to Gretchen. "Here"

"I'm not a big fan of semi-auto's," she said quietly.

"Just until we get back to your guns, okay?"

She nodded and took the pistol.

The rest of the guns were in the duffle bag, which I slung over my left shoulder. The ammo bag was nestled in the bottom making the not light bag more awkwardly bottom heavy.

Gretchen was wearing a pair of Nike's a pair of jeans that seemed baggy at the bottom but tightening the higher they went. She had a t-shirt with a picture of a cat seemingly smiling. She had traded out her leather half jacket – which was now in the duffle –

for a denim jacket, which at some point had been bedazzled, but the effects had started sheering off with time. The design which at one point must have been geodesic or symmetrical was now just a glittery disarray of pasty jewelry.

I had my underarm holster, but the P-30 was stuck in the back of her jeans, covered by the jacket. As random as her outfit seemed when she picked it, she wore it well.

We walked a few blocks before getting on a bus and riding huddled together on a seat with the duffle stuck between the window and us. We got off in a sleazy part of town because we felt we'd draw too much attention in a nicer part of the city. We walked from the bus stop till we saw the flickering pink neon of a sign reading *Motel* that the sign Vacancy flickering. There was an additional sign reading, "Very Clean – Under New Management." From the outside, it had the feel of being somewhere on the spectrum between *Feel free to cook meth here* and *Cash Only, Room by the Hour,* or *Your Husband or Wife will never know*.

The night clerk definitely looked like he smoked meth that probably didn't get made here anymore. His pants were too big, his shirt was too small, and his ball cap seemed too small for his head.

"Hey Doug." I put on a fake smile as I set the duffle down by the counter.

"Who's Doug?" The guy asked in a voice raspy enough to smooth wood.

I pointed to the patch on the shirt that read *Doug*.

"I'm Steve," he said in confusion.

"Does Doug know you have his shirt?" I asked. I hadn't expected this exchange to be this intriguing.

"Who's Doug?" he asked again, as if the record had skipped.

"Room for the night," I sighed before adding, "please."

"It'll be twenty cash for the hour." he said as he started scribbling in a ledger.

"How about for the night?"

He thought for a moment, then checked a laminated list behind the counter. "Twenty-five."

I dropped a crumbled ten and a twenty on the counter. He gave me five one's back that from the glittery state they were in told me they'd spent time in a thong at a strip club. He pushed the ledger over and I scanned the names and knew most of them to be fake. I signed Samuel Spade. He handed me the key with the burgundy diamond shape bob whose number had faded but could still be felt as #5. I hefted the duffle.

"Thanks, Steve."

He looked shocked. "How did you know my name was Steve?"

I pointed to the patch on his shirt. "Doug told me."

As I was walking out I heard him ask, "Who's Doug?"

Gretchen was waiting outside and slipped her arm in mine as we walked to room #5.

The once shag carpet was flattened, the old 20-inch tube tv sat on a dresser whose laminate layers were starting to peel. There was a small round table by the window and door whose orange top convinced me it'd come from a Hooters. The bed was a double and sagging in the middle. The lamps on the nightstand were mismatched. The mirror by the sink and counter was cracked. But the bathroom was amazingly, shockingly clean.

I pushed the door shut and set down the duffle. "I've stayed in worse." Gretchen nodded in agreement.

She walked to the phone. "Wanna order a pizza before the places stop delivering?"

"Sure."

She didn't ask what I wanted but ordered a pepperoni. I'm okay with meats on my pizza, but pizza in its most perfect form is crust, sauce, cheese, pepperoni, and that's it.

"You like pepperoni?" she asked after hanging up.

"It's my favorite." That made her smile.

We sat and pulled the guns from the duffle and started reloading partially spent magazines with the ammo from Saul's. I added fresh batteries to the Tac-Light in the MP-10. I checked and made sure the folding stock locked when extended; it would not be great if it started collapsing on you as you're trying to take the recoil.

"Do we have a plan?" Gretchen asked as she loaded 9mm rounds into a magazine. We had more ammo than we needed... right then, anyway.

"Surviving not a plan?" I was afraid that had come out flippant, but it came out roguish. I got lucky on that one.

She smiled. "Surviving is a state, not a plan."

"Well, I'm open to suggestions."

She thought for a moment. "Well, two things pop to mind."

I loaded the topped up 10mm mag into the sub machine gun and dropped the bolt, making sure the weapons safety was on then checked the Tac-Light. It worked as well. "Wanna share?"

"Well, I think we need to know more and that means one of two things. We either have to find out what the Heaven's Hotdogs know, which means getting someone who knows something, Or..." She paused longer than a classic Shatner pause. "Or, we have to find out what my people know."

"Wanna just call them up?" I chuckled.

"I really wish it were that easy."

"I'm with you on needing to know more." I sat the submachine gun down. "But at some point, we need to make sure Jammer and Joy are okay."

She nodded and looked concerned.

"I'm sure they're safe," I assured her.

"Think they're hiding out?" she asked. That made me laugh.

"What?" she pressed.

"Nothing."

"Tell me." She leaned in with concern.

"Seriously, you don't want to know."

"But I do." Now her tone sounded playful.

I looked into her big, dark, liquid eyes. "If it's up to Jammer, he's probably banging the bottom out of Joy with an E-Y right now."

Gretchen gasped, then covered her mouth with her hand to cover her smile but in the couldn't hide it from her eyes.

I chuckled. "It's awkward as fuck, right?"

"Well, I did think they'd hit it off." She spoke slowly, like she wasn't sure she approved of what she was saying.

"Well, you're battin a thousand on that one."

She laughed.

The pizza arrived, and we hid the guns under the comforter before opening the door to pay. I tipped the driver the five glittery ones I'd gotten as change earlier, then I went and washed the body glitter off my hand and prayed it wasn't all over the inside of my pocket.

Gretchen had started digging in as I pulled off my jacket and shoulder rig. She had stepped out while I was cleaning up and had came back with four cans of Dr. Pepper. She smiled mischievously.

"I love Dr. Pepper," she said.

"Me too." I lifted a can. "Know what the main active ingredient in Dr. Pepper is?"

"Prune Juice!" She answered like an over excited contestant on a game show.

"Yep," I agreed. "So you know what that means?"

"What?"

I held up the can, the logo facing her like they do for product placement in movies. "This is the healthiest thing in my diet."

She was sipping as she laughed and then held her hand over her face as she slowly set the can down. "It came out my nose!"

I laughed as I watched her go to the counter and clean up with a hand towel. She took off the denim jacket and sat back down. I picked up my can. "So, what are we drinking to?"

She clinked her can to mine. "Good days, good company, new friends."

"*Slainte*." We sipped, but our eyes never unlocked.

The pizza wasn't great, but it was good enough and would eventually come out all right in the end by tomorrow. Even sleeping nine hours form the Fentanyl, it had been an exhausting day. I'd have never imagined at my mother's funeral that I'd be eating pizza with the hottest stripper to ever grace the stage at Sharky's after having been in a car chase and a gun fight. I chuckled.

"What?" she asked around a mouth full of pepperoni and cheese.

"This is probably one of the top three days of my life."

"Best?"

I shrugged. "At least noteworthy."

"Oh yeah, what's done it?"

I thought about everything: funeral, car chase, gunfight, getting shot...

"You."

She blushed. "Me too."

We ate in silence for a while. Our eyes would meet and then we'd glance away, embarrassed. The situation would have been simple for me had Bruce Campbell not told me she's my damned soulmate. If she were just the hottest woman I'd ever met I'd be trying to sleep with her. Instead, every time I would look at her my mind would wander then I'd hear Bruce telling me, "Don't fuck it up."

"What?" she asked after a while.

I knew I couldn't tell her, so I decided to try and change the subject. "You said two things. Gather info and what's the other?"

She chewed and swallowed before taking a slow sip of Dr. Pepper. Her eyes didn't meet mine as she nonchalantly tossed out there in the most conversational of tones. "We should have sex."

I was in mid-bite and immediately started choking. I had the horrible flash that I was gonna die choking on cheap pizza in front of my soulmate without getting to have sex with her, all because I hadn't gotten my food down before she told me that's what we should do. My epitaph was going to be "Nick Decker, the dumbass who came so gloriously close."

She got up and patted me on the back. "Need the Heimlich maneuver?"

I shook my head as my throat worked, finally getting it down. I gasped a couple of times before looking up to her as she smiled down to me. "What?"

"We should have sex." It was the simple, matter-of-fact way that she said it; it was a statement without nuance or any complication. It was the manner all men wished women communicated in and then when it did happen, it was like a punch in the gut. There was nothing simple about it.

"I mean if you don't want to..." she began, back-pedaling.

"No it's not that. It's... well..." I was stumbling over words like a kid over untied shoelaces.

She put her soft hand on my shoulder. "What?"

"I don't want to fuck this up." I said it too fast, but at least I said it. A day ago, I wouldn't have been afraid of fucking things up. A day ago, I would have just said "damn the torpedoes" and ran with it.

"Isn't that the point?" She presented herself like the model at the end of the runway. I looked at her, trying to not screw it up, but I was still a guy.

"Seriously."

She smiled softly. She stepped close and reached up to touch my face the way an art fan touches a sculpture or guys like me touch a really cool gun.

"Why?" she whispered.

"Cause your kinda fuckin perfect and that's goddamned terrifying." Sometimes you lie, and sometimes honesty is the best policy.

"Why?" She spoke even softer now.

"Because I don't want to fuck this up. I don't want to be me, and you end up gone. I don't want to make you leave, Gretchen." My voice cracked. "I don't want to fuck this up."

She reached down and lifted my chin. It wasn't until then that I realized I was looking at her feet.

"Then don't."

That was the moment when we should've kissed. My eyes locked to hers and I blurted: "Bruce Campbell said you're my soulmate!"

"Huh?" Of all the things she expected to hear, that probably wasn't near the top of the list.

I took a breath and tried to speak slowly. "Bruce Campbell said he was our guardian angel, both of us... because we're soulmates. And he told me not to fuck it up."

She laughed as she slid in my lap wrapping her arms around my neck. "Then don't."

Some people regret the things they've done in their life. That had never been me. I had lived in constant fear of repeating and regretting things I didn't do. I'd rather get something wrong than miss it. As Teddy Roosevelt put it, I'd rather fail daring greatly, or in my case in mediocrity, then never to have tried at all.

She leaned in and I knew three things: This was the best day of my life; I wasn't going to regret what I didn't get to do, and lastly, some people are great at sex.

I know my strengths, and I was about to leave my soulmate sexually disappointed.

XV: A Secretary as Good as the Title of the only Vertical Horizon Song I Could Remember

I have never been stellar in bed. At my peak I could be liberally described as adequate. I heard someone once say sex was a marathon, not a sprint. With Gretchen it felt like both. It was like being as good as you were in a dirty dream you had as a teen after falling into a porn hole while at the same time it seemed as if everything I had ever failed at with others had been simply saved in a capacitor for Gretchen. There was nothing I wish had done different; there was nothing I would have changed.

She lay against my side breathing softly into the crook of my neck and shoulder, as I had my arm around her with an intensity of a man who was afraid life's tide was going to tear what he had away from him. Was she that good, or was my life that shitty she was just that good in comparison? Is that what soulmates were?

I held her and we slept. We woke and came together again, and again the next morning. We showered together, which was awkward and playful at the same time. I stood in the back as she let the water cascade through her hair. I watch the rivulets of water drip down her back and arms, gliding down the crimson and gold feathers of her tattooed wings.

The view she got was nowhere near as nice.

We dressed and gathered our things. We didn't check out, instead we simply left the key in the door and walked away. I had stayed in five-star hotels before but the last night had been the best I ever spent in a hotel. Beyond the obvious, I am not kidding when I say I slept better with Gretchen there with me than I had in all my life. No dreams, no nightmares... just blissful rest. I, for the first time since learning how fun alcohol was, woke up without even the threat of a hangover.

We'd discussed the plan in the shower and decided that we needed cash. I had twenty-five hundred stashed in my office. We knew it had to be being watched, but we weren't seeing a lot of options.

We hopped a bus and rode until we came to the neighborhood my office was in. There was a second-hand shop where we went in and got some longer jackets. I found a tan trench coat that screamed *I'm a goddamned Dashiell Hammett character!* and Gretchen found a dark blue all-weather jacket that came down to her knees.

In the alley behind the shop Gretchen slid the sawed off double barrel under her new jacket. I slung the collapsed stock MP10 under my left arm, grip forward for a cross draw and tugged on my new Sam Spade coat.

We stopped in Mac's Liquor and Sundries where I tended to buy my scotch. Earl, the guy who ran the shop, said he'd watch the duffle without any questions asked. Thus unencumbered and armed to the teeth, we headed to my office at 505 Gavin Drive, office B-3. The building had been built in 1919 before the Great Depression and had done business since then but never really thrived. I kept waiting for the day I got the notice that I had to vacate because they were tearing it down to build some yuppie condos or an Urban Outfitters next to a Douche Bag Hipster Mustache Salon. I didn't know if Douche Bag Hipster Mustache Salon was a real thing, but it sadly wouldn't have shocked me.

We came in the lobby and Gretchen admired the classic, detailed tile floor. I headed to the stairs. The elevator worked, or at least that's what the building inspector said, but I didn't trust it.

Whoever numbered the building was a moron. First floor was 1. The second floor was A, and the third floor was B, and so on. Why numbers weren't used was beyond me. The only thing I could think of was, "Let's piss off Nick Decker." But as much as I bitched, I could afford rent here, so I kept my trap shut.

I shared the third floor with three other businesses. The first was Claire Daughtry's Photography, which occupied B-1. Claire was a sweet lady in her early 60's who ran a small studio and did her own processing in her office. Every Christmas she would bring everyone the floor pies except for me, she brought me cookies. I don't like pie. It's a texture thing. B-2 housed a failing travel agency. In the past three years it has had four different owners who brings in new crews with every change. The Internet has fucked their profession, but this office hasn't really seemed to notice yet. B-4 was Cleveland Guthrie, CPA. Cleve was a one-man show. No secretary or crew except in the two big tax seasons, business in October and regular people in April, when he would bring in assistants. Apparently, he made enough in October to run the business and keep himself afloat the rest of the year. Cleve was my accountant and ran my account for free because I got the photos that got him a divorce without alimony.

B-3 was an oak door with a powdered glass window bearing the simple stencil of *Decker Investigations*. But as Gretchen and I came down the hall, it was obvious the window had been smashed out and the door left hanging on one hinge with a busted bolt.

I pulled the MP10 out from under the coat and extended the butt-stock, bringing it to my shoulder. Gretchen had the sawed-off at the ready. Without hesitating, I flowed through the door and button-hooked along the wall, clearing the corner before quickly scanning the room with the barrel of the sub machine gun.

It scared the hell out of Agnes.

I couldn't tell you if Agnes had dark blonde or light brunette hair. She was twenty-four and had been working for me since she was twenty. She dropped out of high school at age sixteen and had gotten her GED. She then took night classes and got associates in something or other by the time she was eighteen. She had left her last job when her boss offered some non-kosher suggestions to improve her job performance. I couldn't remember what her associates was in; all I knew was she typed the way Usain Bolt sprinted and she organized like a Lego master builder with chronic, debilitating OCD.

The place had obviously been tossed, but Agnes's desk was already placed back into immaculate working order, with the exception of the broken desktop monitor and smashed computer.

Yesterday morning I would have told you Agnes was my type; buxom, tall and sweet. But that misconception had been corrected by the short, dusky mischievously humored stripper who followed me though the door with a sawed-off shotgun going straight along the wall, covering the corner as opposed to button-hooking with me. Agnes screamed, but as opposed to the Wilhelm Scream of the movies it was a violent, clipped yip.

I lowered the sub machine gun and put on a smile. "Morning, Agnes."

She held her hand to her chest for a moment, then regained her composure. "No messages, Mr. Decker."

"Thanks. What are you doing here?" I looked about the ransacked office. It was a two-room office suite, three if you counted the bathroom. The front room held Agnes's and my desks. The back room, which was more accurately described as *the room to the left*, had a pullout couch, a small flat screen TV with an Xbox 360, a fridge, a kitchenette, and a door to the small bathroom complete with small shower stall. I lived in the room to the left. The closet in the main room belonged to the place where Agnes hung her jacket or coat and storage for office supplies. The closet in the room to the left belonged to my cheap off-the-rack suits.

"Office hours are eight to five pm with the eleven to twelve hour shut down for lunch." She repeated it rote, like an ad she read in the paper.

"You're not worried about—" I gestured at the wrecked office, "all this?"

"I assumed it was just an angry subject of investigation." Like she sounded about everything else, her tone was completely matter-of-fact.

"Did you call the cops?"

"No." She sounded incredulous. "You're a private investigator. Why would you need a government-funded investigator?"

Gretchen laughed. "She's kind of got you there."

Agnes nodded matter-of-factly. "Thank you. She then stood, smoothed her dress and came around the desk, now completely nonplused about the firearm in Gretchen's hand. Agnes held out her hand politely. "Welcome to Decker Investigations. I'm Agnes."

Gretchen smiled and shook Agnes's hand. "I'm Gretchen. I'm with Nick."

Agnes nodded politely. "Very good, Ma'am. If there's anything I can assist you with, please don't hesitate to let me know how I can be of any service."

"Thank you so much." Gretchen smiled. I started moving to the back room. Things were too sweet in the office.

My pull-out couch was wrecked, the small safe had been smashed, the TV had been kicked in and the Xbox 360 had been stomped. My kitchen looked like I imagined a hipster's face would look after calling Connor McGregor a gender-fluid Englishman. My admittedly cheap suits had been ripped and slashed. Someone had left an upper decker in the bathroom. My bottle of Macallan 18 was smashed. It was the smashed bottle that hurt the worst. I don't make a lot of money and that heavenly concoction isn't cheap.

I found my tool bag scattered over the floor and fished a Philip's head screwdriver out of the mess. I walked over to the closet door and opened it. For a second I wondered why I'd looked for the screwdriver when I could have just used the Gerber in my pocket, then I decided thinking about it was giving the problem more time than it deserved. I knelt and start undoing the hinge from the door. Gretchen came in and crouched over the remains of the Xbox 360 and began working.

I got the three screws removed and moved the hinge. In the door there was a block I fished out with my pocketknife revealing a slick, which is basically a cool term for a little hidden space. I dug my Gerber pocketknife in and hooked the edge of the wrapped envelope and dug around until I could get my fingers on it and pull it free. I opened the envelope and thumbed through the bundle of cash before slipping it in my pocket.

"What are you doing?'

She looked up and came up with something I didn't recognize but knew I should. "It's the xBox 360 memory, this way you don't lose your achievements!"

My jaw dropped. "You... are fuckin amazing." What kind of girl thinks of something like that at a time like this?

She laughed and playfully slapped her own denim-clad ass as she stood pocketing the memory unit.

We got the guns back under our jackets and then stepped back into the office.

"Agnes." She looked up attentively and magically pulled out a pad and pen to take notes. "Call a cleaning crew to get this place straightened up and the door fixed. Then forward all calls to one of the cells in the desk that still work and go home. It's not safe here. Work from home until I tell you otherwise, all right?"

"Cleaning crew," she jotted down. "Forward calls, work from home. Anything else, sir?"

I reached in my pocket and fished out the digital point-and-shoot camera. I popped out the memory card. "Yeah, on your way home drop this by the law office of Garvey and Burns. It's for Ms. Garvey. She'll know what to do with it, and don't leave until she gives you the check."

She scribbled on the pad and stood. She calmly took a phone from the desk drawer and set up the forwarding before she walked to the closet and retrieved her coat. "Have a good day, sir."

I walked to the remains of my desk and got a new memory card for the camera and slapped in a fresh battery.

We made our way down the steps in the silence of footfalls.

"What now?" Gretchen asked as we made the lobby.

"Now we go get some answers."

She smiled, maybe it was the determination in my voice making me sound authoritative and inspiring or maybe she thought it was cute. "Where?"

I thought about the bag of guns, and the fifteen-year jail sentences Gretchen and I were carrying under our coats at that very moment. I smirked.

"Peaches. We're finally getting our sit down with Peaches."

XVI: Sit Down with Peaches

Peaches ran a van company that did farm to restaurant produce delivery. They had a warehouse down by the docks, not because that's close to farms, but because it was cheap. His real name was Gary Tucker III, but that's not the name you picture when you imagine a former high school point guard who was closer to the seven side of six and a half'ish feet. He got the name Peaches because the first illicit shipment of guns he ran he hid in crates of peaches. Twenty years later, his legitimate business made enough money to live comfortably; it was his illicit business that allowed him to live like a garish asshole.

A good salesman will tell you that they'll pay more attention and put more effort into a customer who walks in wearing cut off BDU shorts, a t-shirt, a pair of Wayfarers, a chain tucked into his shirt, and a scratched Rolex than they would a customer who comes out dressed to the nines with precious medal chains on display and a polished, immaculate Rolex. The reasoning is odds are the second guy is trying to show off how much he has; the first guy has so much he doesn't care. Peaches is the second kind of guy.

He stood at the window of his office looking down over his warehouse where fruit and veggies were organized for delivery, fresh and never frozen, with the occasional bit of guns tossed in. He wore an immaculately tended white linen suit with pink shirt that he would argue is salmon and a white tie bearing the perfect single Windsor dimple. His shoes were polished so bright one could shave using them as a mirror. If history were to play out, he had a four-inch nickel-plated Smith and Wesson .38 under his jacket, a gold plated lighter and cigarette case – filled with menthols for some ungodly reason – and a pair of gold-rimmed eye glasses.

You couldn't call Peaches because he didn't carry a phone. Instead of dropping money on the newest iPhone or Samsung, he had a nineteen-year-old kid named "Gravy" who carried a collection of burner phones in his pockets. Gravy did triple duty as Peaches secretary, bodyguard, and being an all-around ass hat.

Gretchen and I stashed the duffle of guns and ammo in a dumpster. I stuffed my trench coat in the bag as well. I would have liked to walk in there with the 10mm submachine gun, but it wouldn't be diplomatic. However, Gretchen kept her all-weather coat though with the sawed-off shotgun and HK P-30, and probably Jammer's .357, because I didn't see that in the bag.

"You can wait here if you want," I suggested. I didn't know how hairy things were going to get and I couldn't decide if I wanted her there if the shit hit the fan. I knew she was good in a fight, but if something happened to her…

She smiled. "Your hand is on fire."

I looked down and saw that yes indeed, my right hand was burning. I shook it and the fire extinguished without burning my sleeve or suit jacket.

She stood there with a bemused look. "That's the second weirdest thing about you."

"What's the first?"

"You speak German in your sleep." She slid her hands in her pockets as she shrugged. "According to the files, you don't speak anything but English. So that's weird."

I shot her an offended look. "I speak fuckin Pig-Latin."

She reached up and patted my cheek patronizingly. "Okay."

I reached under my jacket and thumbed back the hammer on my .45 that was being held by the leather strap that was under my left arm. I knew it was ready to go — checking was just a nervous twitch.

I offered her my left hand and she took it as we started walking. "You really should have sunglasses," she told me.

"They got smashed back at the office."

We walked thought the large roll up doors as a nondescript panel van pulled out. Even though all the vans had "Farm-to-Table Express" painted on the side, they screamed, "Hello little boy. Would you like some candy?"

We moved along the wall out of the way of everyone to the stairs that would take us upstairs to the office area. I could see Peaches at the window in his white suit and bald ebony head so shiny it had to be waxed. There was a stooge at the bottom of the steps dressed in a Hilfiger polo outfit like he was the villain in a 90's teen drama. He put his hand on my chest as if to say *I could push you if I wanted to but I'm being polite in order to be intimidating*.

I pointed to the office with my right hand as Gretchen gave my left a reassuring squeeze. "Go tell Peaches I can get his alimony killed so all he'll have to do is pay child support."

The goon took this information and looked up the stairs, then to me three times. In his head he had to be calculating, *Boss said he didn't want to be disturbed, but if I fuck this up it's my ass*. Finally, he made the right call, or the right call for me anyway and took us up the stairs. The office was decorated by a person who thought he understood sophistication but didn't.

"Hey, Peaches." I said jovially as the two goons at the door shut it behind us. They didn't check us for guns. I wouldn't have been surprised if they had. They were armed, we were armed, detente. However, we were experiencing the courtesy of Mutual Assured Destruction.

"So, you can get rid of the alimony?" His voice was deep and felt like burlap overfilled with gravel. His back was to us.

"No," I admitted. "That was just to get in here."

He turned and glared at us through his round, mirror-refracting John Lennon sunglasses. "So what's to keep me from throwing you out the bloody window?"

Bloody window... I wondered when Peaches started putting on airs of being British.

Peaches leaned his hands on his desk. "Jammer set up that meet for you later today?"

"Yep."

"The fuck you want, Decker?"

Peaches thinking he could intimidate me started to piss me the fuck off. I stepped forward and felt the goons behind me tense up. "Who the fuck is arming the goddamned Heaven's Hotdogs and where was the gear delivered to?"

Peaches grimaced. "Watch the blasphemy."

My eyes narrowed. "Fuckin' hell..." I muttered as I spun, drawing my .45. I shot the first goon in the middle of his forehead blowing his brains back against the wall behind him in a bloody splatter. The goon on the other side of the door I caught in the throat with a bullet and then just to the left on his chest with the second, causing him to slump back against the wall grabbing at his neck as his life was ending. Holding his neck like that coupled with the chest wound was simply bailing water on the sinking Titanic with a spoon.

I kept spinning to get back around to Peaches. The roar of Gretchen's double-barrel blasted out the windows behind Peaches but he'd ducked down out of the way as he saw her come up with it out from under her coat.

I heard Peaches grunt and flip the large wooden desk. I put two rounds into the desk top facing me not knowing if they had punched through or not, but I wasn't waiting around to find out. I was running toward the desk aiming along the lip until I could see a target. Gretchen was working around the side but keeping an eye on the door.

She heard the door start to pull open from the outside and gave the door the second barrel from the sawed-off. Outside we heard Hilfiger goon scream.

Peaches came up with a Tec-9 in each hand. I shot him in the gut with my .45 ACP spit from the barrel of my 1911. He stumbled backwards grabbing at his gut without dropping the guns in his hands.

I vaulted his desk. Gretchen opened the breach of the sawed-off and held it under her arm as she aimed the P-30 from the hip at the door and started reloading the sawed-off with her free hand. Goddamn that was sexy.

I grabbed Peaches stupid tie and jerked on it pulling him forward then punching him in the chest causing him to stumble back towards the broken window. "Talk mother-fucker!" I barked. "I've seen wounds like this — you can live through it if you don't fuck around." I saw the black blood on the white suit. I was lying about him making it.

"Name Gloria Patris Et Vexillifer." He prayed as he looked to the ceiling. Tears streaming down his cheeks from under the glasses.

I aimed the 1911 and shot him in the foot. Peaches crumpled onto the floor as his foot gave way, but I kept a hold of the tie. "English mother-fucker!"

He looked up. I could see my reflection in his glasses. "I can do all things through Christ who strengtheneth me."

Behind me Gretchen whispered, "Philippians chapter four, verse three, in the King James version."

Angrily I pressed the 1911-barrel to Peaches left elbow and pulled the trigger. He screamed.

"You gave them the guns, Peaches." I'd figured that out by now. My 1911 was empty and the slide was locked to the rear. I dropped it and punched Peaches in the gut. My hand came away bloody from the wound. "Where are they?"

Here is the thing about interrogation. Torture can get you bad Intel. But since the gunplay started it became a time issue. With Peaches liver shredded, it was a time issue doubly so. But here's the other thing about interrogation, everyone breaks. Everyone... eventually.

Peaches reached up and tore off his sunglasses. Fear and pain filled his eyes but I could see the glowing in the reflection of his dark eyes. I heard the fire crackle. The Fiery Sword burned in my right hand.

"Name Gloria Patris Et Vexillifer. Name Gloria Patris Et Vexillifer. Name Gloria Patris Et Vexillifer..." he repeated over and over.

I was pissed and getting more so by the freaking second. You shoot someone three times, you expect some answers. I pressed the tip of the blade to Peaches left ear and got the whiff of pork BBQ as his earlobe cauterized away. "WHERE?"

"Corner of Canal and... and... Merchant. I met him at Canal and Merchant." He cried, and it felt good.

"Met who?" I growled.

"*Zadkiel!*" He screamed, because I was digging the tip of the burning blade in his knee. The stench of melting polyester over rode the pork barbeque smell of burned human flesh.

I let him go and picked up my 1911 with my left hand and stuffed it in the waist of my suit.

"You better make peace with whoever you're talking to, Peaches. Because you're gonna meet him in the next fifteen minutes." I bent and picked up one of Peaches TEC-9's and started walking to the door with the Fiery Sword still burning in my right hand. The door opened outward, so I kicked it by the knob. Hilfiger goon lay clutching his right arm which was peppered with shot from the 12-gauge and splinters from the door.

He looked up at me in terror and I pressed the flat of the burning sword to his left sleeve, slowly started to smolder and slowly tendrils of smoke started to rise. The sword burned in my hand and I don't think I'd ever felt so goddamned mad before in my life.

I don't think I'd ever felt so righteous.

Hilfiger goon's sleeve caught fire. He flailed his arm trying to put it out. I pushed my foot into the center of his chest letting him burn. I leaned in close and growled, "When the bastards show up, and you know who I'm talking about, tell them Nick Decker is getting tired of their bullshit."

XVII: I Don't Speak Latin, Either

People ran as we were leaving. The Fiery Sword burned in my hand and as I walked I kept touching things, setting them on fire. I've never been one of those guys who get an erection when they light things on fire but at that moment, I could see the appeal.

I stabbed the blade through a van window setting the seat on fire. As I walked away the rest of the interior started going up as well. By the time I left the warehouse eight *Farm-to-Table* Express vans were engulfed in flame. The working crew had scattered. I looked around with a maniacal desire just wanting someone to fight; I wanted someone to fuck up. I wanted the goddamned world to burn.

Gretchen had a worried look on her face. "Nick, we gotta go. If the Peaches crew doesn't show up, the Heaven's Hotdogs will, or the cops."

"Let'em fuckin' come!" Spit flew from my mouth as I snarled. I thought I saw movement and spun raising the Tec-9. I loosed one shot and blew a brown rat in half. I've never been that good a shot.

I saw the parking lot and started walking toward it and cooking off a round with the machine pistol with every step. Every shot I fired shredded the tire of a different car. Soon the magazine ran empty and I tossed the gun. I grabbed the pommel of the Fiery Sword with both hands and the blade grew from two feet to four feet and the grip elongated to comfortably fit both hands.

"*Nick!*" screamed Gretchen.

"THE FUCK DO YOU WANT FROM ME!" I roared and took a step toward her. The sword was raised above my head.

Gretchen's eyes were wide, and her lip trembled. "Nick... you need to stop." There was fear in her voice. Fear for me or of me?

I felt something tugging at the back of my mind, trying to get attention. I felt a simple, pure need. "I need..."

She stepped closer. Part of me wanted to take the burning blade in my hand and chop her beautiful fucking head off. In the words of Metallica, I wanted to kill'em all.

"What do you need, Nick?"

I felt a smile grow on my face. It didn't feel natural, but it felt good. I felt the thing in the back of my head tug harder. "I need... kill em all... I need to burn it all." I looked to her. "I need to burn the goddamn world, Gretchen."

She was close. She reached out and took my face in her hands. Her touch was soothing, like aloe on a fresh sunburn. She leaned up as she pulled my head down and kissed me. I let go of the sword with my left hand and took her cheek in my palm as my lips opened to hers. Her tongue danced playfully with mine. I let go of the pommel with my right hand and pulled her into my arms. The Fiery Sword was gone as I held her tight to me.

I don't know how long the kiss lasted, but quality wise, it was one for the record books.

Her lips slowly parted from mine.

"Gretchen," I whispered. "God I'm sorry..."

She held my face and smiled. "It's okay."

"No, it's not." I could feel it in the back of my head, or was it the memory of the rage?

She nodded. "I think it was the sword, not you, Nick."

"If you weren't here..." I whispered because it was all I could manage.

"Shhhh." she soothed. Her hand felt perfect as it held my cheek. "I was," she said softly, then her voice grew lovingly adamant. "...and I will be."

I pulled her tight in my arms and held her there as the warehouse behind us burned.

"We've got to go." She took my hand and we started running back to the duffle.

I dropped her hand and pulled my 1911 from my waistband and reloaded it before lowering the hammer and sliding it back in my shoulder rig. I pulled the bag from the dumpster and slung it over my shoulder. We moved until we found a street with cars parked along it and Gretchen stopped at an old 1983 Dodge Omni hatchback. She deftly popped the lock and hot-wired the car. I threw the duffle in the back and climbed in the passenger's seat.

She got us on the road and I opened the duffle, grabbed rounds to reload my empty magazine.

"I'm not sure," she said slowly as we made the corner, "that this particular trip was worthwhile."

"We learned a little."

"Corner of Canal and Merchant. I'm guessing it's a warehouse or a clubhouse for the Hotdogs." I felt her smile. It was the smile of a person doing a puzzle and they just found a corner piece.

"What was that Latin shit he was saying?" I asked with quiet curiosity.

"I don't speak Latin," she confessed.

"There was something familiar about it." I was racking my brain, trying to figure out what.

"Really?" She looked at me confused, but she also looked like she was wringing her brain to see if something she'd forgotten fell out.

I nodded. "I've heard it before, or seen it." I pulled my phone out and thumbed back through the pictures. "Name Gloria Patris Et Vexillifer"

"That's what he was saying," she agreed as we turned onto Broad Street.

I held up the phone. It was the tattoo of the dead Heaven's Hotdogs. She repeated out loud as she read. "Name Gloria Patris Et Vexillifer." She smiled. "It's not a lot, Nick."

"No, it's not," I agreed, putting my phone away. "But it's a connection. And sometimes a connection is all you need."

She reached over and squeezed my hand that held hers. "So do we have a plan?"

I shrugged. "We have a notion, that's better than we had a few minutes ago, right?"

Gretchen laughed but it was a nervous laugh. I must have really scared her earlier. If I were to be honest, I was freaked out about it as well.

"I'm tired of knowing less than these cocksuckers."

She nodded, seeing where my mind was headed. "Okay, so who do we know?"

"I dunno." I know I did know *someone*, but for some reason I couldn't think of who so "I dunno" seemed the safest answer.

"We could always use Google Translate," she offered.

"Yeah, then we'd know what it means, but I think we need someone who knows and can explain *why* it means what it does."

She nodded as she drove. "Would Jammer know someone?" Gretchen asked helpfully. "He's your Guy for that Guy, right?"

I squeezed her hand and pulled it to my lips to kiss it. That brought a genuine smile to her face. "Gretchen, you're a freaking genius."

She smiled and shrugged nonchalantly. "Well obviously. I'm a woman of intelligence, high morals, and exquisite tastes."

I laughed. We'd met in a shady strip club and the only meals we'd shared together were finger foods and a pizza. "That you fuckin are, my dear."

Finding Jammer wasn't as easy as calling him up or showing up at his place. After last night he would have gone to ground. He carried burner phones, but he would have tossed it the second he went out the back with Joy with an E-Y. He wouldn't be at his place until he was sure he wasn't being followed. However, I knew a couple places he might be.

Gretchen suggested we start with Joy's place. We started there but it was obvious no one was home. We went by the Titanium Lighting club where Joy worked but her manager said she'd not checked in, however she wasn't due a shift till tomorrow, so that wasn't unusual.

While we were there the manager offered Gretchen some stage time. Even with a sparse Wednesday lunchtime crowd, in the space it took the speakers to play Theory of a Deadman's *Bad Girlfriend* Gretchen made seventy-two bucks. The pigtails she tied her hair up in and the schoolgirl uniform she removed probably didn't hurt anything.

She came out of the back in the beat-up denim jacket we'd got her at the second-hand shop, but she'd traded the jeans for dark grey yoga pants, a black studded belt that reminded me of the collar a villain dog would wear in a cartoon, and a belly uniform shirt that belonged to an employee at the local Hooters.

Her all-weather jacket and my trench coat were in the back of the stolen car with the guns as we drove. Jammer kept an efficiency apartment by the bowling alley; not the fancy bowling alley, but the one whose restaurant menu was *Hamburger $1.50, Hotdog $1.00, Chips*, there wasn't a price for chips. I'd always wondered about the chips.

I knew Jammer had a sister who would put him up if need be. We drove by her house; her kids were off at school. The signal would have been the flag on the mailbox being up. It was down so we kept driving without even stopping. I didn't want to involve Christina in anything.

I knew there was a shady motel down by the river where Jammer kept some emergency gear stashed. In the air vent for Room #5, there was an envelope with some cash and a 9mm Walther pistol. We parked there and went inside. I asked the clerk, a sweet old lady who deserved better business than she got if she had any available rooms. She said they all were available. I thanked her, and we walked out leaving her even more disappointed with life.

We drove by the self-storage where Jammer had a storage garage and kept a small RV stored under a fake name. This was where we got our first real break. The RV was gone. He'd bought the RV after watching Breaking Bad but he'd never made drugs in there, Jammer just took it on road trips and to the lake sometimes when he wanted to get away.

We spent the next five hours driving around the perimeter of town. There was a state park and several KOA style campgrounds to check. We found the RV at a KOA.

We drove off and hid the duffle in the woods by a road sign, then went a few more miles down the road. We pushed the car down a broken, abandoned boat ramp into a swampy morass where it started to sink. We didn't wait for the end.

The walk back to the KOA was pleasant. The weather was nice enough in our coats. We left the duffle where we'd hidden it and went on to the camp. I stood with my arm around Gretchen as I knocked on the camper door.

It took a minute before the door opened and a shirtless Jammer popped his head out. He didn't seem surprised to see us in the early evening.

"Oh, hey." He didn't add, *what took you so long!* but it seemed implied. Before we could say anything, he continued: "Can you come back in like twenty minutes?"

From inside we heard Joy with an E-Y's voice call out languidly, "Jam-Her...!"

"Maybe thirty?" he corrected. Without waiting for an answer, the door closed.

We stood there staring at the shut door. From inside we could hear the familiar music of a dance with no music.

Gretchen looked at me. "Are they—"

"Yep." I answered, not really wanting to know how she was going to phrase the question.

"I'm glad to see they were worried about us." Her tone was a juxtaposition of deadpan and light-hearted.

"Yeah," I uttered with all the deadpan snark I could muster while attempting to not sound like a dick. "Their concern for us is moving… like the quality of emotion actors win Oscars for."

"That's just what I was thinking," Gretchen agreed.

"Should we walk away before the little RV starts rocking?" I asked.

She sighed. "God, yes."

Arm in arm, we turned and walked to the small clubhouse office of the park. We used some of Gretchen's stage earnings to buy two cans of Dr. Pepper and two personal sized bags of Nacho Cheese Doritos and a pack of Nutter-Butters to split. I carried everything, and we walked to a bench overlooking a pond.

We ate our junk food and sipped our drinks quietly. The sounds of nature were ruined by the sounds of RV people grilling and laughing and talking, but it wasn't bad.

"Can I ask you something?" Gretchen said as she looked to me with those large, liquid dark eyes.

"Hit me."

She paused and chewed her chip noisily. "What are we?"

I thought about that a moment. I'd been thinking about that already, so really another moment didn't help. "Calling you my soulmate feels weird and calling you my girlfriend feels infantile."

"Yeah," she agreed. "Like we're in middle school passing notes." She did a mocking tone. "Wanna be my girlfriend? Check yes or no."

I laughed. I finished my bag of Doritos. "Holy shit!"

"What?" She looked around scanning.

"I know who would know… I know who to ask about the Latin shit."

"Who?" Her eyes were alight.

"My Uncle."

"Your Uncle?" she repeated skeptically.

"Yeah, he's the coolest guy I know. Knows all kinds of weird shit. He's like if Indiana Jones had a baby with Frank Sinatra, Uncle Lew would make fun of that kid for being lame. And the kid would believe it, because that's how damned cool Uncle Lew is."

My eyes met Gretchen's and it's safe to say I fell into them. I reached up and wiped my fingertip over her nose, smearing Dorito dust. I laughed, she laughed, and we grew a few steps closer.

Maybe we were infantile enough for boyfriend/girlfriend.

XVIII: Friends Like These

Everywhere we sat in the RV left me wondering, *how long ago did they have sex right here?* Joy sat wearing one of Jammer's t-shirts and with the height difference, it didn't quiet cover her midriff. She had a blanket wrapped around her waist and it left me praying that she had something on underneath it. Jammer was wearing boxers and a grey t-shirt with the sleeves cut away. Both of their hair were in disarray but Joy had more hair to be disarrayed, so it was far more obvious, but Jammer's looked far crazier.

"So," Gretchen said slowly. "What have you two been up to?"

"Don't answer that," I blurted before anyone could say anything.

Joy blushed, and Jammer seemed to wink with his whole face and somehow his left shoulder.

"So, uh..." Jammer offered, "glad you're not dead?"

"Was that a question, Jammer?" I asked.

"Maybe?" His eyes were wandering like he was watching butterflies that weren't there, or simply that we couldn't see because they existed someplace he was at and we weren't.

"Maybe?" Gretchen repeated.

"Well," Jammer gestured between him and Joy. "We may be on a little acid..."

"And a little weed, and a lot of ecstasy," Joy added ever so helpfully.

"So," Jammer continued, "living in a bicameral universe where a statement had to be either declarative or interrogative really isn't where we are right now. We're kinda gliding in an ethereal realm where positive and negative coalesce and pop-rocks live in harmony with soda."

Joy stared at Jammer in awestruck wonder. "You are so effing smart." She grabbed his bearded face and kissed him.

I looked at Gretchen and she looked to me so we didn't have to look at anything else going on.

Joy climbed up and straddled Jammer then pulled his face to her t-shirt-covered chest. "You're like the wise old wizard at the rainbow mountain top." With the blanket now in disarray, it was no longer a mystery what was or was not under it.

Gretchen and I nodded and started to get up, moving to the door.

"Jammer," I called out without looking.

"Yeah, Nick?" His voice was muffled as his face was buried in Joy's chest.

"Pick us up by the first road sign heading back in town, okay?"

"Okay," his muffled voice agreed.

Gretchen got the door open and we got out but not before hearing Joy with an E-Y scream, "USE YOUR MYSTIC WAND, SORCERER!"

"Our friends are weird," Gretchen whispered as she clung to my side as we walked away from the RV.

We got the duffle bag and waited about an hour before the RV pulled to a stop. Jammer and Joy were in the front seats and both seemed truly clothed this time.

"Hey you two," Joy called out. "Hop in!"

It was when we climbed in the back we noticed neither of them seemed to have pants on but neither of us examined how much or little was being worn beyond that horrific surprise.

"So, what's the plan?" Jammer asked as we got back on the road.

"We've gotta go talk to Uncle Lew."

Jammer completely took his eyes off the road to look back to us. "I love Uncle Lew, man. That's just the coolest dude." Luckily Joy grabbed the wheel and kept us from crashing. When Jammer turned back around she took her hand off the wheel and set it in his lap.

Gretchen and I pointedly didn't pay attention.

"So why did you come find me?" Jammer asked after a bit.

"We needed someone to help with some Latin shit," I said, keeping my eyes on Gretchen. It quickly felt that she was the only safe thing to look at.

"But your Uncle Lew—" Jammer started.

"Yeah, I forgot about Uncle Lew till we'd already found you, dude."

'Oh." Jammer nodded and drove. "Okay." He accepted that answer as logical.

We rode for a bit before Gretchen looked to the front and grimaced. I didn't want to know what she saw.

"Jammer," she said far more calmly than I thought I would given the circumstances, "I've got your .357. You can have it back."

"Oh, thank you." Jammer seemed really grateful. Maybe it was because Gretchen was giving his gun back, maybe he was grateful for something else. "Did you kill anyone with it?"

"I did," Gretchen said slowly. I think she didn't want to sound proud.

Jammer chuckled. "That's awesome."

We drove into town and stopped by a parking structure. Jammer looked back. "You two wait outside." I took the duffle and held the door for Gretchen and we stood outside the RV. I had expected Jammer to drive off but after about five minutes, the back door opened, and Jammer emerged. He wore baggy cargo pants and a t-shirt under a reefer jacket along with a grey tweed driving cap. He walked up and opened the passenger side door and said with a caring tone, “Drive, stay at little camp sites, use the cash in the glove compartment and don’t come back until I call.”

Joy sat in the driver’s seat with tears in her eyes. “Okay.” She looked to me. “Take care of him, Nick.”

I smiled. Well, it was more of a smirk. “I try.”

Jammer shut the passenger door and Joy with an E-Y drove away in the small RV. He watched in silence until it was out of sight. Without looking to Gretchen and me he asked quietly, “Can I have my back-up pistol back, please?”

Gretchen pulled out the revolver and handed it grip first to Jammer. He checked the cylinder and then slid it and the speed loader into his ankle holster.

“Jammer?” I asked.

“Yeah, buddy.” He was quiet, wistful even.

“Why didn’t you go with her?” I had hoped he’d go with her. I don’t like putting my friend’s dicks in holes when I didn’t know what was on the other side.

He looked to me and I’ll be honest, the look stung. He seemed hurt and betrayed. “Because you used chivalry to send me out the back at Asian Karaoke. You’re in some shit and I’m not going to live the rest of my damned life knowing I wasn’t there for my best damned friend.” He pointed in the direction of the RV, which had disappeared into the distance. “She’s safe. And now I got your back.”

There were tears in Gretchen’s eyes, and I crossed the distance between us to throw my arms around Jammer. A man hug; a warriors embrace. Three pats with the non-gun hand then break. There were tears in Jammer’s eyes too.

“So,” Jammer said as he wiped his eye on his sleeve. “What’s the plan?”

“Well, I’m guessing someone is probably watching Uncle Lew so we gotta figure out how to get close.” I scratched my head doing nothing to fix or make more of a mess my unruly hair.

“He still at the crazy rich dude compound?” Jammer asked.

I nodded.

“There will be a couple ways in.” When Jammer sounded confident it was infectious.

Gretchen sounded pleased. "Need me to get a car?" she asked, gesturing at the parking structure.

Jammer laughed. "No, I got some wheels in there." He nodded appreciatively. "But it's cool you can do that."

We climbed the stairs of the parking structure. I went first, Jammer last. As scumbag-ish as we can be at times, chivalry died hard between us. It was the fourth level of the structure where we found the dark blue '95 Toyota Camry. Jammer had hidden the key inside the front driver's side wheel well. I opened the door and popped the hood and the trunk. Jammer walked to the trunk and took out the car battery, carried it to the hood, lifted it while resting the battery on his knee then rehoused and connected the battery. He dropped the car hood and gave me a thumbs-up. The car engine turned right over.

I tossed the duffle bag in the back seat and climbed in the driver's seat; Gretchen took the passenger's seat and Jammer climbed into the back.

Jammer grumbled as he buckled up into the middle seat in the back. "My car… why am I riding bitch?"

We pulled out and paid the weekly rate for parking out of Gretchen's Titanium Lightening money. Jammer was good about keeping his hides and safe houses paid and stocked. The long-term parking ticket we paid was for only three days. It felt a little strange, for the first time since going to Little Saigon Mega Awesome Disco Karaoke we were riding in a car that couldn't be described as "hot."

The radio presets had all been messed up when Jammer disconnected the battery, so Jammer had removed his seatbelt and had wedged his torso between the front two seats as he reprogrammed the six radio presets. He picked two classic rock stations, one contemporary station, one country station, one rap station, and NPR. The process was painful because he would pass a station three times looking for "the perfect frequency" before programming it as a preset.

"Just hold the button, Jammer," I growled as he dug his elbow into my thigh to hold him up.

"I gotta get the right freq, Bro."

"Jesus Christ, Jammer! It's a digital display... you're not turning goddamned knobs. You know what the station is, just go to it and set it." I reached up and turned off the windshield wipers, which he had just turned on with his shoulder.

He managed to get his elbow in my crotch before he was finished. Gretchen laughed, I found it less than amusing. Jammer slid back into the back seat and buckled back up.

"Put it on the rock station," he called out. Gretchen hit preset #1. "No, the other one," he corrected, and she complied. "So why are we going to Uncle Lew's for?"

"Why are we going for?" I asked, "Or did you mean, '*What* are we going for?'"

"Okay," he said huffily. "You can answer what I mean or pay attention to what I say. Either way, you don't have to be a dick. *What* needs translated?"

I sighed. "What needs to be translated? Shit, how high are you right now bro?"

I glanced back in the rearview mirror as he held up his left thumb and forefinger, but the distance between them from touching to about an inch and a half. "Medium High?"

Gretchen turned in her seat and looked back to him. "High enough to believe you're a stand-mixer?"

He laughed. "That's funny. Stand-mixers are funny. The beater is too big to lick, like you know, mom's do when they make cakes. But how awesome would that be?"

Gretchen reached back and patted his knee. "It would be real awesome."

"We should make a fucking cake!" Jammer exclaimed. He was off topic, but I knew he'd eventually come back to us so I pressed on.

I took out my phone and flipped to the pic of the tattoo and handed it to Gretchen, she in turn held it out to Jammer. He took the phone and looked at the picture, then started pressing the screen. A minute later, he said, "For the glory of the Father, capitalized by the way, and of Bearer, also capitalized. Google Translate for the win!"

"Okay, buddy," I said calmly as I turned onto the interstate. "But what does it mean?"

"Fuck if I know," he confessed.

"Okay, you know anyone that might know?"

He thought for a moment. "Your Uncle Lew might." Gretchen smiled back to him and he reached up shaking both hers and my shoulders. "Oh my God Uncle Lew is the coolest guy."

"I've heard," Gretchen said, smiling sweetly. It was like a Mom smile just before she pulled candy from her purse. Good candy; not some bullshit butterscotch.

"Nick!" Jammer gasped with a glee. "Did you tell her who he looks like?"

I shook my head.

Gretchen turned sideways in her seat and looked at me curiously. "Is it anybody in particular?"

"No," I said calmly.

"DUDE TELL HER!" Jammer cried.

I sighed.

"Tell her or I will," Jammer huffed.

I looked to Gretchen and she smiled curiously. "Gary Oldman," I told her, and her face lit like a Republican's erection when you mention abolishing the estate tax or a Democrat's when you say Universal Healthcare. "He looks like Gary Oldman."

IXX: Uncle Lew

It was early evening by the time we got to Uncle Lew's. I didn't call because by this point, I was paranoid enough that I assumed he was being watched too. Paranoia can be an interesting emotion. As long as you're not sitting around with tinfoil on your head and crotch in order to block out the space-based mind control lasers, it could even be a useful thing. Paranoia only has to be right once for it to all be worthwhile.

For most of the ride Jammer sat sideways in the back seat watching behind us. We got off at exits we didn't need to, sometimes to simply get back onto the highway immediately. Not getting followed isn't about driving like a character in a car chase movie; it's basically about driving like an asshole. With both Jammer and me in the car, we possessed an abundance of asshole.

Early in the ride Jammer did a bump of cocaine and that really evened him out. I never did drugs. I mean, I used to drink like a fish when I was younger, but that's not the same thing. To be fair, I still drank too much by any clinical definition. My definition of a alcoholic, boozehound, one with a drinking problem, etcetera, was someone whose drinking affected their work. So I guess if the same definition could be used for drugs, Jammer was square too.

Jammer sat with the Franchi SPAS-12 on his lap. Gretchen had the sawed off handy. If a horde of Heaven's Hotdogs numbering like the Mongolian horde turned up, we'd at least make a splashy showing.

Anti-climatically, the ride was clear and uneventful. I found myself looking to Gretchen next to me and Jammer in the back seat. I found myself thinking of my little brother. He probably wished for a better relationship than we had and though I reasoned that might've been nice, I knew it wasn't practical. He'd spent too many years being too big a piece of shit for me to ever respect him. I've made plenty of mistakes in my time on earth, but at least I wasn't that asshole. Blood said he was my brother, but that's it.

Then there was Jammer in the back seat. Coming off acid and ecstasy with the help of a little cocaine. But he was there, shotgun in hand, ready to do violence on behalf of a cause no greater than his friend. Has there ever been a greater cause than that?

I looked at Jammer and Gretchen. Long ago I realized a simple truth we figured out in the army but had forgotten in the mediocrity of the real world.

Two types of family exist: the family you'd go to hell for, and the family you'd go to hell with. It doesn't take a mathematician to figure out which had the greater value.

My life was a road map of poor life choices but looking at the company in that car I wouldn't have changed a turn. I'd like to think that if the situation were different I'd have Jammer's back just the same.

We parked a ways off and walked in. I had the 10mm submachine gun under the tan coat, Gretchen the sawed off under hers. Jammer, lacking a long jacket, put the SPAS-12 in the trunk with the duffle and stuffed the extra P-30 9mm in the back of his pants.

Uncle Lew lived in the middle of nowhere. Instead of walking down the road we stayed inside the wood line with Jammer leading the way. Jammer's ability to Land Nav was preternatural. He'd left the 82nd Airborne to go to Special Forces Selection. The Star Course, the culminating exercise for selection, is arguably one of the hardest land navigation courses in the world. Jammer, as the story was told to me, looked at the grid for his point, looked at the map, stuffed both in his pocket and started running. He made it to his next point, looked at his new grid, looked at the map, and started running again. He repeated this process until he finished, at which point he strung his poncho liner up with 550 cord into a hammock and took a nap, having basically run a marathon over broken ground.

He wasn't in that kind of shape anymore, but his Land Nav game was on point. It was dark by the time we got there but that was nothing to Jammer. We got to the wall of Uncle Lew's, for lack of a better word, compound, without ever coming in sight of the road. We worked our way around the back. Out front was a large vehicle gate, but in the back was a small double-layered pedestrian gate so he could go on walks or I guess, thinking tactically, escape.

There was a small call box, I hit the button then looked up to the dome security camera and waved like a childish asshole.

Uncle Lew was freaking rich.

We didn't wait five minutes. We heard the inner gate open then the outer swung out toward us and there he stood with a flashlight in hand.

"Nicholas!" He smiled jovially and while making sure the light wasn't in our faces he moved and wrapped me in a hug.

I patted his back and gave him a squeeze. "I've missed ya, Uncle Lew."

"This is such a lovely surprise." He let me go and looked to the others. "Jammer my friend." He moved in and wrapped Jammer into the same warm embrace.

"How's it going Uncle Lew?" Jammer gave Uncle Lew a squeeze and then another.

Uncle Lew looked to Gretchen with a broad smile. "Jammer, you gotten yourself a girlfriend?"

Gretchen giggled, and Jammer laughed. "No, she's with Nick."

A surprised look dawned on Uncle Lew's face. His was a face of juxtaposition, ever expressive, and ever sphinx like. It's like you could always read Uncle Lew but never understand him.

He stepped forward and held out his hand, palm half up. *"Bonjour ma petite beaute, he dirais que tubes le visage d'un Angel, mais qui ne te rendrait pas justice."*

Gretchen blushed and held out her hand. He took her fingers between his fingers and palm gently and lifted her hand kissing her knuckles gently.

"I'm sorry, I don't speak French." She sounded bashful, not the confident stripper who ruled her stage with impunity.

"Do you speak any other languages?" Uncle Lew asked Gretchen.

"I'm a polyglot." When she told me this same bit of information she sounded proud, but now she seemed embarrassed. "I speak Vulcan, Klingon, Dothraki, and Sindarin."

Uncle Lew smiled and leaned close to her half whispering. *"Hello nin dilthen beautui, im would ped- cin are i visage -o an aenil, butthat would u- ceri- cin justice."*

Gretchen blushed.

"What the hell was that?" Jammer asked.

Gretchen looked up to Uncle Lew with large, amazed eyes. "Sindarin."

"What the hell is that?" Jammer asked, nearly the same question.

"A language created by J.R.R. Tolkien for his race of elves. I do believe it's phonology is close to Icelandic, but I think it's more Welsh than anything." Jammer might be my Guy Guy, but Uncle Lew was my 'Knows Weird Shit Guy.'

Uncle Lew smiled. "My apologies. I just have a hard time believe an angel as lovely as you would have her eye taken with our Nicholas." Uncle Lew's voice and manner would be cloying if it weren't for the fact that he was both somehow sincere and playful.

I groaned. "Thanks Uncle Lew."

Gretchen smiled. "It's hard to explain, but there's just something about him." Thank God she didn't say: *we're soulmates.* Because that would have sounded batshit crazy... wouldn't it?

Uncle Lew looked to me. "Are you going to introduce me to this angelic visage or should I choose a name for her?" He glanced back to Gretchen. "I would name you Helen, a face to launch a thousand ships and worth beginning the greatest war in history."

"There have been bigger wars," Jammer offered.

"Bigger, yes Jammer," Uncle Lew said, smiling, "but not greater."

"Uncle Lew," I offered. "This is Gretchen."

"Milady." Uncle Lew smiled again. "Pearl in the Greek."

Jammer laughed. "Do you know what every name means?"

"Jammer fits better than your given name, Michael, but I do believe it comes from the Hebrew for *who is like God.*" Uncle Lew then smiled to me. "And *Nick* is something his father thought of while shaving." That got a laugh from Gretchen and a belly laugh from Jammer.

"Well," Uncle Lew said quietly shutting off the flashlight leaving us in the near dark of the star filled night. "I'm sure you came to this entrance for a reason, and I'm sure it's a good one. Let's get inside, shall we?"

Jammer lead the way through the gate, then Gretchen and I followed. Uncle Lew came last, securing the gates behind us. Uncle Lew then pulled out a small walkie-talkie and thumbed the mic. "Stennis, could you please re-arm the Ped Gate and reactivated Camera 3, please."

The walkie-talkie squawked. "Yes." A pause, then, "Set. Full perimeter has been re-established. Is there anything else you require?"

"That's nice of you to ask, Stennis. Could you inform Barnes that we have guests. We'll need two rooms prepped... and inform Mrs. Barnes we will require some refreshment in an hour. Nothing heavy." Uncle Lew offered his arm to Gretchen. She took it and they began leading us along the gravel path cutting through the well-manicured lawn.

"You don't have to go to any trouble, Uncle Lew." I told him as I followed with Jammer.

"It's not for you, Nicholas," he said, looking back at me over his shoulder. "I'm simply being a good host for the lady and my friend Jammer." He leaned in close to Gretchen and mock-whispered, "Of all my nieces and nephews and such, Nicholas is my favorite, for he is the least trouble and doesn't accept gifts, or as he puts it, *charity*.

But I don't have children of my own, so I think it's rude of him to not let me dote." He gestured to the large house behind him. "I'm not exactly hurting, as you can see."

Gretchen looked back at me and then back to my uncle. "May I ask something...?"

"You, Milady, may ask anything you like," he assured her.

"Why is he your favorite?" Gretchen asked suspiciously, not believing the answer he'd already given her.

He grinned charmingly. "He's the most like me."

We got to the elegant French doors which opened into the main entranceway from the rear, between the curved set of stairs. He paused and smiled down to her warmly. He leaned in and whispered something I couldn't hear but I saw the smile on Gretchen's face. He had to be lying. Nothing about me should be able to make a woman smile like that, even if she was my soulmate.

Uncle Lew opened the doors and held one open for Gretchen. We all entered. Inside on the black and white marble floor under the chandelier waited Barnes in his immaculate tuxedo with his hands clasped politely behind his back. Barnes was tall and gaunt, but not cold and severe in the way you'd assume a man with his stature would be. He was in his early sixties and his hair was a regal gray and pomaded tight to his scalp. He was an official member of the Guild of English Butlers. His voice was a rich tenor that must have been trained on the Shakespearean stage. His was the voice meant to be the Prince in *Much Ado About Nothing*, or in his younger days, MacDuff in *Macbeth*. As long as I'd known Uncle Lew, I'd known Barnes. When we had come to Uncle Lew's as a kid Barnes snuck me candy from time to time. He's also taught me to pick a pocket, which raised some questions, but none worth offending the gentleman by asking.

He half bowed. "Misters Pinero and Decker, welcome back to Sheol house."

Jammer flushed. I think the last time anyone had referred to his last name was the first and only time he'd been here, and it had also been from Barnes.

Barnes bowed to Gretchen. "Milady, welcome to Sheol House. I am Barnes, the butler. If there is anything I can do for you do not hesitate to let me or any of the staff know. If anything is not satisfactory let me know immediately any time, day or night."

A young, no more than twenty-one years old housekeeper in traditional English uniform came with a small silver tray and tongs. She took them and lifted small, rolled white towels, offering one to each of us. The towels were damp and cool and smelled lightly of citrus as we each took one and wiped our faces. Jammer really used his to scrub his beard. I was embarrassed by how dirty my towel was after I worked it behind my ears.

When we were finished the housekeeper took the used towels and placed them on the tray with the tongs.

"*Gracias*, Esperanza," Uncle Lew said. He then looked to us. "All of you, and by this I mean no offense, look a little worn. Barnes will take you to rooms. Feel free to shower or relax in the tub. There are robes in each closet and Esperanza will see your clothes are cleaned." He pulled a gold fob watch from his pocket. "At this late hour I'm going to insist you stay the night. But I don't think you'd have come if it weren't important. So, should we meet in the study in an hour?"

I looked to Gretchen and Jammer and we all nodded. "Sounds good, Uncle Lew. Thanks."

He gave me another hug and Barnes began leading us upstairs. At the top of the curved stairwell as we turned into the hallway, Gretchen leaned into me to whisper. "God you were right." I looked down with raised eyebrows and she clarified. "He *does* look like Gary Oldman."

XX: The Devil You Know and The Devil You Don't

Gretchen and I ended up taking two showers in the time allotted by Uncle Lew. We undressed and left our clothes in a pile. I hung my shoulder rig and the MP-10 from hangers in the closet. After we had showered and came out wrapped in towels, we found Esperanza had already collected our things and was gone. Our eyes met.

We had sex on the large four-poster bed. It was something in a realm that existed between fucking and lovemaking. After this, we took another shower more for courtesy for everyone else than a need. I finished first and came out and found a robe in the closet. There were two; a thick Egyptian cotton black one, and a white silk one. The black one was longer, so I took it and got lost in the warmth and softness of it as I wrapped it around me tying a simple overhand knot in the thick cord of the same fabric.

Gretchen came out of the bathroom with a thick towel wrapped around her torso and another one in her hands drying her hair that made ravens seem pale.

"Nick," she said through the mass of hair and towel as she dried. "Don't take this the wrong way, sex with you is great..." I didn't believe it, sex with me has never been great for anyone. "but I might trade you for the steam-setting on that shower in there if that were an option."

I laughed and pulled the white robe off the hanger. I walked over and held it open for her as she tied the towel around her hair the way that girls do and let the towel around her torso drop to the floor.

I stole a look and felt no guilt or regret about it. She turned, and I saw the red and gold wings tattoo going from her shoulder blades and down. God knows how many hours she lay on the table for those, but the work was immaculate. "What's with the wings?"

She looked back over her shoulder and smiled. "You like 'em?"

I laughed. "Who could find something to bitch about when it comes to you?"

She grinned. "When I was a kid my Mom told me the only thing that kept me from being an angel was I didn't have wings."

"What about a halo?" I asked as I traced my finger along the wings painted into her skin.

She laughed lightly as she tugged the robe up and tied it in place. "Didn't seem anything more than a detail." She looked back over her shoulder to me mischievously. "The Queen of England is still the Queen of England even if she's not wearing any headgear, right?"

I chuckled. "Headgear as in orthodontics or civilian for hat?"

She stuck her lip out playfully as she pretended to think. "Civilian for hat. I hated when my parents made me wear orthodontic headgear."

"You've not mentioned your folks before, they approve of you being all Secret Organization-ish?" My eyes locked to hers. It was like staring into pools of infinity and finding something meaningful at the middle of it all.

Her face darkened a bit. "Dad's gone, but Mom is a Sister of the Order. That's how I got in."

I didn't push, and she seemed to appreciate that.

"Well, speaking of angels, I didn't tell you at Karaoke—"

"Asian Karaoke," she interrupted. It was half-spoken, half-giggled.

"Goddammit." I sighed, then, "I was gonna say you have the perfect Mezzo Soprano of an angel but fuck it."

She grinned and put her hand on her cocked-out hip. "Now Mr. Decker, I get the feeling that came from Jammer, not you."

"Why would you say that?" She was on to me.

"While you were knocked out we chatted and what-not. He's actually a really good piano player." She sounded a little amazed at that.

"Nope I knew that, about voices and such." I was sticking to that story.

She smiled. "Bullshit." How did she make that word seem sexy?

We slipped on our provided house shoes, which matched our robes and headed down to Uncle Lew's study. We found Lew and Jammer waiting on us. Jammer's robe was a battleship gray. Uncle Lew was wearing a cream suit that was made more for the tropics and a white shirt with no tie. I got a lot of my style from Uncle Lew.

He was standing at a decanter and pouring glasses. On the table was a tray of shrimp and various sauces, a tray of southern style – yes, there is a goddamned difference – fried chicken and biscuits, a tray of quiches, a tray of various fruits, everything from apples to dates, and dips.

"If I remember correctly," Uncle Lew said with his back turned to us, "in terms of Scotch, Jammer is a sixteen-year Lagavulin man, but Nicholas, like myself, is a Macallan drinker. However, on this occasion..." Uncle Lew turned around. "Jammer, would you substitute your go-to Scottish delicacy for a twenty-five-year Macallan?"

"Sure. Thank you," Jammer said around a mouthful of shrimp.

Uncle Lew poured the scotch into crystal tumblers. He then looked to Gretchen. "My apologies, Milady. I don't know your beverage of choice."

"I don't want to be trouble."

He smiled. "I insist, trouble me."

His smile was infectious, and she caught it. "An Old Fashioned?"

Without missing a beat, Uncle Lew began mixing. He took an old-fashioned glass and began muddling the bitters, sugar, orange rind, a cherry, and splash of soda. He then removed the orange rind and gently poured bourbon into the glass before adding a ball of ice using tongs. He garnished it with a fresh rind of orange and a fresh cherry.

He brought our drinks over on a silver tray. There was a small pitcher of water with a glass pipet for adding a drop of water to our scotch. Uncle Lew picked up a glass and held it up. "A toast, to friends new and old."

We picked up our glasses and clinked them to Uncle Lew's. The half-Wop half-Mick Jammer and me, the scotch Irish American mutt, simultaneously said: "*Slainte*." Gretchen said nothing until she sipped her Old Fashioned.

"God, that is delicious!" she gasped.

"God had nothing to do with it, my dear." Uncle Lew smiled. "That concoction is all me and good bourbon." His eyes then turned to me with a gravity my usually lighthearted Uncle rarely displayed. "So, what brings you here, Nicholas?"

I felt the robe and sighed. "Shit, I left my phone in my jacket pocket."

Uncle Lew reached the table and rang a silver bell. Barnes quickly appeared in the doorway. Uncle Lew addressed him ever respectfully.

"Barnes, would you be so kind as to retrieve Nicholas's phone? It should be with everything that was in his pockets."

"One moment, sir." Barnes disappeared and reappeared moments later with the phone. I retrieved it from him and came back. Uncle Lew and Gretchen were already sitting on the couch and Jammer had taken a chair. I pulled up the picture of the tattoo and handed it to him.

I sat in the other chair across the food-laden table from Uncle Lew and Gretchen.

As he studied the picture, Gretchen got my attention and directed me subtly to realize that my legs were spread and I was in a robe. I tried my best to subtly shift and push the robe for modesty's sake.

Uncle Lew sat the phone down. "Well, the literal translation is 'For the glory of the Father and the Bearer."

I nodded. "Yeah, that's what we got from Google Translate."

"What do you need from me?" Uncle Lew asked as he sat back on the couch.

"Context." Coming from Jammer that could have been a declarative or an interrogative statement. Coming from me it sounded like a demand.

Uncle Lew nodded. "Well, first off, this is all supposition and mythology, okay?"

I nodded. I must have picked up my knack of nonverbal communication from him as well.

"I think 'The Bearer' it must be referring to is Zadkiel." He spoke slowly as if he were coming to grips with what he was saying as he was saying it.

"Who is Zadkiel?" I asked as I sipped my scotch. I love the 18 Macallan; it's expensive, but it's what I buy. The 25 year was as out of my league as Gretchen.

"He is the banner man of the armies of Heaven. That's why he's referred to as 'The Bearer' here. So, the question is, Nicholas," he asked as he sipped his scotch, "what does this have to do with you?"

Gretchen chimed in with deft political acumen and courtesy. "These people who have this tattoo think Nick is carrying around the Fiery Sword."

Uncle Lew didn't seem shocked or seemed to think that this was particularly crazy. "I see." He turned his eyes to me. "That would be something, if the stories are true."

"What stories?" Jammer asked, stuffing another shrimp in his lips.

"Well, according to Genesis, it was left at the Gates of Eden after the expulsion of man." Uncle Lew spoke like a kind college lecturer, but not in the classroom, but more like at a bar with his favorite students. "But there are stories that say that it wasn't just man that was expelled, they say that the expulsion of man was also the expulsion of the devil, as well."

"But didn't the devil try and overthrow God in the beginning?" Gretchen asked.

"Well," Uncle Lew said reasonably, "what if it was subtler than that. What if God did have a plan, but the devil cocked it up with free will by convincing Adam and Eve to exercise their own, so the expulsion from the garden coincided with the expulsion of the devil from the presence of the Throne."

"What's that got to do with this Zadkiel dude?" I asked.

"Not dude," Uncle Lew corrected. "Archangel. How do I explain this?" He paused a moment, gathering his thoughts before continuing. "Okay, think of a Jazz ensemble. A bunch of instruments held together by a conductor or band leader, right?"

"And God is the band leader?" Jammer suggested in an interrogative form.

"No." Uncle Lew smiled. "The Father is the patron, the venue owner. The first angel was the bandleader. He kept the choirs in harmony, on the music so to speak, but when he's expelled from the Presence of the Throne, what happens?"

"Who leads the band?" Gretchen asked.

Uncle Lew clapped his hands together. "Exactly! Now you have a bunch of musicians, all still playing, but trying to direct at the same time. Gabriel the messenger, Michael the warrior, Zadkiel the banner man... this is what the expulsion of the devil did, it put the band in disarray."

"So why would they be after Nick?" Jammer asked.

"Well, how do you choose who is the most important in that situation?" Uncle Lew leaned forward, his tone was a mix of college lecturer and skald.

"You mean with angels?" I asked.

Uncle Lew nodded.

"Who is the most divine?" Gretchen offered.

Uncle Lew smiled. "Oh, I like you. Yes. That's why they'd be after the Fiery Sword."

"Huh?" That was Jammer.

Uncle Lew paused and ate a slice of pear and sipped his scotch before continuing slowly. "Let us look at this like a logic exercise."

He stopped until he saw three agreeing nods. "Why do you think God is benevolent and loving?"

"Cause he's God?" Jammer offered.

"Okay," Uncle Lew nodded in agreement. "Why then isn't man for the most part? Was man not made in God's own image?"

"Because we're not perfect. God is omnipresent, omnipotent and omnibenevolent," Gretchen offered, "Right?"

Uncle Lew smiled. "Someone knows their St Augustine of Hippo. Let's table that for a moment and look at the concept of the Trinity."

"God the Father, God the Son, God the Holy Spirit?" Jammer offered.

Uncle Lew held up his hands in a golf clap. "So if God can be all three, why not a fourth?"

"Huh?" Jammer exclaimed as his jaw dropped at the thought.

"Man isn't wholly benevolent and loving because man has rage. What if the Fiery Sword, isn't a Sword?" Uncle Lew offered Socratic-like.

Bullshit it isn't a sword, I thought as he continued.

"What if the Sword is a metaphor, or even the actual incarnation, of the unfettered Wrath of God? What if after the fall, or the falls, God separated himself from his Wrath, or at least the majority of it, for the betterment of his creation?"

I thought about the want, the drive to burn the world that I felt tugging at me at Peaches.

"If you could separate a negative aspect of yourself from yourself, would it be better to leave it to whither, or set it to a task, something useful?" Uncle Lew continued.

"Like guarding the Gates of Eden," Gretchen muttered. Her eyes met mine. She also remembered me at Peaches. She was smart enough to extrapolate what I could have done had she not been there.

"Precisely." Uncle Lew got up and refilled his tumbler.

Jammer piped up now. "So whichever angel gets it gets to be the new bandleader because it would mean they're closer to God than the others. Is that what you're saying?"

Uncle Lew nodded.

"Why wouldn't demons be after it as well?" Gretchen asked.

"Maybe so far the devil's kept them in the dark," Uncle Lew suggested.

"Why would he do that?" Gretchen pushed.

"Well, we know from Genesis the devil can walk the earth." Uncle Lew held up a finger. "We know from Job he can go to the Throne." He held up a second finger. "And logic is clear that he can go to Hell." he held up a third finger. "So, the devil spends his time in three places. Think about Armageddon and what it means. It means this..." He gesture broadly around the room. "All ends, and there is only Heaven and Hell. So in Heaven, the devil is a pariah."

"The butt-monkey," Jammer said seriously.

"An apt analogy, given tropes," Uncle Lew agreed. "At the Throne, the devil is the butt-monkey. Hell is obviously Hell, so it can be reasonably assumed as unpleasant. As opposed to Earth, where, though not perfect, is better than the alternative, correct?" He gave us a moment and let that sink in. "Why would the devil want this to end? And why wouldn't the archangels?"

There was a long silence where the only sound was the tick tick of the grandfather clock in the corner.

"Sooo," I know I sounded skeptical but there was a great reason for it — I was. "You're telling me an archangel is sending bikers to kill me to get not a weapon, but the actual Wrath of God?"

"Pure and unbridled." Uncle Lew nodded slowly in agreement.

"Not to be out of line, Uncle Lew," I said, "but how the fuck would you know?"

"Weeell," he really drew that word out. "There are ancient cuneiform tablets talking about things like the Ananaki, tablets in Ancient Greek and pre-copper age artifacts, apocryphal books of the Bible that didn't make the cut at Nicaea, the Akkashic record..."

"The website in the weird part of the Internet?" Jammer asked.

Uncle Lew touched the tip of his nose with a finger on his right hand and pointed to Jammer with his left hand.

"I told you it was real!" Jammer shouted and slammed back his 25-year-old scotch like it was a shot of Jägermeister at a bachelor party.

I watched Uncle Lew. I'd known him my whole life. In all the weirdness of the past few days, he was really the only constant of my life from before. Something felt off. He'd always had a cool adventurous lifestyle, a mix between Indiana Jones and some super bookworm.

I don't remember asking as much as I remember hearing myself asking. "Who are you, Uncle Lew?"

He looked down in his drink and smiled softly. "Are you sure you want to know? Are you sure you don't already know?"

His eyes met mine and I nodded. I knew, but I didn't believe, those are two separate things. I needed to hear it.

With a charming smile he shrugged and said:

"It's true, your mother was the twenty third demon kicked from the Presence of the Throne. She stole the Fiery Sword when the first drops of rain started falling and Noah became a sailor." He chuckled to himself and held his arms out to his sides in mock surrender. "I'm the Devil you don't know, and the Devil you most assuredly do."

XXI: The Fuck?

The names flowed through my brain like the words to a song that you recognized but couldn't name, or lyrics you knew but couldn't remember the tune.

In freaking alphabetical order:

Beelzebub

Lucifer

Mephistopheles

Old Scratch

The Devil

Uncle Fuckin' Lew.

He calmly sipped his scotch and waited for what had to be the inevitable reaction. But what reaction was inevitable? What's the rational reaction to finding out your Uncle is the devil? I mean, it made perfect sense in a way. He was the coolest person I knew. And anyway, whose uncle is a doppelganger for Gary freaking Oldman?

Shock didn't seem correct. It wasn't shocking once I'd put the blocks together in my mind. They were always there; always had been.

Not surprising, it was Jammer who broke the silence. "Which name do you want to go by?"

Uncle Lew smiled. "I'm fine with Uncle Lew. But if you must, my father named me Lucifer. Your lot came up with the rest."

"Why don't you just take it?" Gretchen asked. "The Sword, the Wrath?"

His smile faded, and he set his glass down. "Because if I have it, it begins. If one of my captains has it, it begins. If one of the archangels have it, it begins." His eyes fell on me. "Everything that is, right now, lies on a scale and if tipped, it will all end. For good or ill, depending on which side of the Judgment Seat you find yourself. The only thing standing between all this and The End is you, Nick. Right now, you and the Fiery Sword, the Wrath of God, are the fulcrum."

"If this ends everything, why does your side want it?" I asked quietly, eyes narrowed.

"Have no illusions, even my most zealous captain knows we can't win a war against the Throne. But—"

There's always a but, I thought.

He smiled. "But some of them, Baal, Asmodeus, a few others, do believe with the Fiery Sword, they can fight to a... how should I say this? A more profitable armistice."

"What about you?" I asked.

"Nicholas," he sighed. "Short of the Father, I am the oldest thing, being, however you want to describe it, in existence. I was the First Creation. Genesis, 'Let there be Light.' That wasn't the sun and stars, that was me." He smirked, and it was odd seeing Uncle Lew, The Devil, seeming self-deprecating. "I know better."

"How can we trust you," asked Gretchen, "after all you've done?"

He looked bemused. "And what have I done?"

"The snake in the Garden of Eden, for one," Jammer offered as another shrimp found its way into his mouth.

"You mean when I said, 'Why not eat from that tree?'" Uncle Lew said, amused. "Did I make anyone do anything? I made a suggestion, and Eve made a choice. Who is the villain there?" It was odd hearing Uncle Lew sound defensive. "In all my time I've only done three things to humanity. I made a suggestion that lead to your kind knowing good and evil, and what's wrong with knowing? How can you have free will if you're unaware of a choice?"

There was a long pause. "Was it an apple?" Jammer asked.

Lucifer shook his head. "Pomegranate. I thought it'd be a good joke. Can you imagine something more disgusting than a pomegranate?"

"They're good for you," Gretchen said.

"True," the devil conceded. "But cut one open and tell me it really looks appetizing."

"And the other two?" Jammer asked in rapt attention. He'd spent years rebelling against his Catholic upbringing, so this was probably right down the middle of his mentally rebellious fairway.

"I made a bet about a man named Job. But all that stuff I did to one man had the Father's blessing. He *let* it all happen."

"And the third?" I asked, wondering what it'd be. The Indians? Armenian Genocide? The Holocaust?

"Then I didn't do anything until 1915," he said with resignation.

"You did WWI stuff?" I asked, thinking of trench warfare and gas attacks.

"No. The Vehicle Act of 1915 was my idea," Lucifer said offhandedly as he waved his hand about before sipping more scotch.

"Huh?" Again, I think it was a simultaneous reaction with Gretchen and Jammer while I muttered, "The fuck?"

Uncle Lew looked genuinely surprised, and then pleased. "It created the first Department of Motor Vehicles. That's on me, but the Holocaust, witch trials, genocides, pedophiles, boy bands, the Kardashians, Rick-Rolling, those are all on humanity, not me."

"But..." stumbled Gretchen, "the devil..."

"What?" he asked with a smile. "The devil put the idea in your head? The devil fed on your weakness? The devil made you do it?" He finished his drink and set the crystal tumbler down. "It must be really comforting to be able to blame me for your kind's weakness and evil, huh?"

Lucifer sat back on the couch and to Gretchen's credit, she did not shy away.

"The best thing the Father ever gave you," Lucifer mused softly, "and the worst thing he gave you, is your free will. Because free will makes it your choice. That means it's on you."

"Sodom and Gomorrah?" asked Jammer.

Lucifer waved his hand absentmindedly. "Your cesspool and Michael and Uriel's clean up."

"The Flood?" asked Gretchen.

"That was the Father," Lucifer admitted. "But you guys really had to push him on that one."

"Christ in the wilderness?" Jammer tossed in.

Lucifer shrugged. "Fasting is stupid, and apparently thinking so makes me the bad guy."

"When I was eight you told me to go ahead and eat chocolate cake before dinner." It was the first time I'd chimed in in a while.

He smiled. "That was Lucifer the Uncle, not Lucifer the Devil. Uncles are supposed to do things like that."

Jammer laughed, then we all laughed. It was that easy.

"So what now?" I asked.

He smiled. "Zadkiel is obviously after you, so it's simple, don't let him catch you. Don't let him get the Sword."

"Is there a way to get rid of it? Hide it?" I asked.

He shook his head. "But it's not all bad, there are advantages."

"Such as?" Gretchen probed, again obviously remembering the affair at Peaches warehouse.

"You're going to find yourself getting better with any weapon you use. You'll find yourself tougher, stronger, healing faster. Stuff like that."

"So the Sword is going to make him Captain America?" Jammer said with a laugh.

Lucifer grinned. "It's not going to change how he looks, but the effect, more or less, yeah." His eyes then fell on me. "It's also dangerous." He looked to Gretchen and reaching over, rested his hand on hers and gave hers a squeeze. "But I think you already realized that, haven't you?"

She nodded.

"Is anyone, anything on my fuckin' side?" I asked. There was a type of desperation in my tone that made me feel ashamed.

Lucifer nodded. "Believe or not, I am. But there's not a lot I can do. I can give advice, but I can't intervene directly. If I do, so will the Father, and then it's over."

That was a kick in the ass.

He continued, "But I get the idea Gretchen and Jammer are on your side."

Gretchen nodded, and Jammer spoke with a grim solemnity. "To the end, bro." Then he reached over and squeezed my shoulder reassuringly.

I could imagine it; Hell on one side, Heaven on the other. Jammer and I standing back to back in the middle ready to die with a "Fuck you" as our last words.

"There's also Bruce Campbell" Gretchen offered.

It was the first time I ever saw Uncle Lew look confused. "The actor?"

Jammer shook his head and reached for even more shrimp. "His guardian angel is Bruce Campbell."

That brought a laugh from Lucifer, deep and hearty. "Oh, that's rich."

"Oh my God!" Gasped Gretchen, then she covered her mouth and looked embarrassed to Lucifer. "Sorry."

He laughed again. "Doesn't offend me."

She looked excited between Jammer and me. "Bruce Campbell, I figured it out." She leaned forward up on her knees on the couch. "We're Burn Notice!"

I could feel my brow furrow in confusion and Jammer looked as certain as an idiot trying to find a word in a dictionary with the argument that you have to be able to spell the word to find it.

She pointed to me. "Nick is Michael Weston." She pointed to herself. "I'm Fiona Glenanne." She pointed to Jammer. "Jammer's Sam Axe." She half turned and pointed to the devil. "And Lucifer is Bad Check Barry the Money Launderer. We're Burn Notice!"

The room was awkwardly silent for a long moment, until the grandfather clock in the corner started chiming. At that point the chime, and the laughter of Uncle Lew shattered the silence.

Gretchen smiled sheepishly as he laughed. He looked to me and slapped his knee. "She's actually your soul mate, isn't she?"

"That's what Bruce told me."

He laughed even more. "Nicholas, I highly doubt that your guardian angel," he gestured between Gretchen and me, "both your guardian angel's isn't really Bruce Campbell. He's as much Bruce Campbell as I am Gary Oldman."

Jammer burst with a mouthful of shrimp. "I KNEW you looked like Gart Oldman!"

"Yeah," I nodded. "Want to explain that?"

"Well, I'll try to put this as simply as I can. If you saw me in my true form, it would wrinkle your brain."

"That sounds scientific..." I muttered.

He continued, unabated. "I had to choose a form. I chose this one because of Nicholas."

My brow furrowed, and Gretchen leaned closer. Even Jammer's elbows were on his knees, legs apart, and modesty a thing of the past in that robe.

"Well, when Nicholas was seven he saw *Sid and Nancy*. I'll be honest, I don't know why his parents let him watch that. And that was just before the first time we ever met. I had to keep my distance because even though Nick's father knew about Nick's mother, that didn't mean he was pleased with his brother-in-law." He grinned sheepishly. "At seven, Nick wasn't in awe with his father and saw me as something as a juxtaposition. Not to brag," he said with a shrug, "but I was cool. As Nicholas kept getting older, he kept watching movies. *State of Grace, Rosencranz and Gildenstern are Dead, JFK, True Romance, Dracula, Romeo is Bleeding*. But it was 1994, with *The Professional* that this form really coalesced because of Nicholas. To put it simply, and not to sound like I'm a genre savvy character in a movie, Nicholas ret-con'ed me."

"Oh," Gretchen said slowly. Obviously she was tracking with the weird meta-conversation.

"Huh?" Jammer answered or asked. That single word could have gone either way.

"Nicholas's father perceived me a certain way before, everyone did. But when Nicholas perceived me as actor Gary Oldman, he inadvertently changed everyone else's perceptions. Not only in the present, but also in the past. Photos changed, memories changed so that this," Lucifer smiled as he held his hands before his face and removed them like playing peek-a-boo, "became the reality."

"The fuck?" I muttered.

"How could he do that?" Gretchen asked curiously.

Lucifer smiled and leaned back, shrugging. "I don't really know. And believe it or not, I know quite a lot."

Jammer reached up and stated to say something, but Lucifer interrupted him with, "Three."

Jammer gasped. "Holy shit. That's what I was thinking! You can read minds?"

Lucifer laughed. "If I want, but you gave it away when you held your hand up. There was a slight curl of your thumb and pinky giving you three elongated fingers, so there wasn't a reason to delve any deeper."

"Seriously, how did Nick ret-con reality around you?" Gretchen asked.

"Well," he sighed, "I think it's because I am, for lack of a better term, amorphous. I am what someone perceives me to be in most cases. Eve saw a snake, after all. I think the Fiery Sword, the unbridled Wrath of God is a small touch of the Throne unfiltered in Nicholas, exerted by his perception on reality. At that point it was simply the universe making sure continuity conformed."

He made everything sound easy. Then again he apparently was the devil.

Uncle Lew reached over and grasped Gretchen's hand. "I can see it. I'm glad you two found each other." He looked to me. "Try not to fuck it up."

"Is that a metaphor?" Jammer asked.

"Fucking it up?" Lucifer asked.

"No, you can see it. Is that a metaphor?" Jammer persisted.

"In a way. Our Chinese friends would say they're bound by the red cord. It's a rare thing. I know this sounds strange coming from me, but I don't believe in miracles. I believe in strings being pulled, things manipulated, random chance made the most of. I don't believe in miracles." He stood still holding Gretchen's hand and then leaned in to take mine. He pulled me to my feet and Gretchen as well. He looked between the two of us kindly. "But I think this rates."

Lucifer let go of our hands and clapped his together and rubbed them. "It's late, we should probably retire. You are safe here. Stennis and his security team have the watch so relax and enjoy yourselves. If you need anything, please inform Barnes." He smiled. "I am really pleased you came to visit." He looked between Gretchen and me. "I'm thrilled you are here."

XXII: The Worst Day Since Yesterday

We slept that night in a king-sized bed with the softest sheets I've ever felt. It was only the second time it'd ever happened but waking up with Gretchen pressed into my side was the perfect fit to a puzzle which before now, had always been missing a piece. Waking up with Gretchen felt like the antithesis of a sad Adele song.

She opened her eyes and looked back to me and our eyes met. I was out of my league. She kissed me like she didn't care, and before I had brushed my teeth even. We got up and showered, shaved, cleaned up, and came back out to the room. We noticed the bed had already been made so there was no more fun on that account; we'd have felt guilty if the maid had to make it again.

We had gifts waiting on us as well. Gretchen was given a pair of black pants so tight they looked like painted on Lycra, a black leather belt with small pouches, and a black tank top with small grey lettering. It was the full lyrics of The Rolling Stones *Sympathy For The Devil.* On top of all this, he gave her leather jacket that looked wet but wasn't and a pair of black jungle boots that were polished to glass. It was simultaneously fetching on her and functional.

I found waiting for me a slim cut two-button dark gray Armani suit with a crisp white shirt that I doubted would ever be that crisp or white again. There was even a new pair of black and white Chuck Taylors. Over this was a long, black leather trench coat that seemed tailored for me.

Downstairs, the breakfast spread was incredible. Smoked kippers, salmon and lox, sausage – both link and patty – hash browns, and on top of that, the Chef Amelie set up an egg, omelet, pancake, and waffle station. There was a container filled with melted butter and another with warm syrup.

Jammer shot me dirty looks, as all I had on my plate was a waffle and a lot of bacon. I wondered what was wrong with a waffle and bacon? The bacon was perfect. Not crispy but limp, the way bacon had always been intended to be eaten.

Jammer had new duds on as well. He was wearing a pair of tan and black Fjallraven hiking pants, Asolo hiking boots, a black t-shirt that had a picture of Han Solo on it that read, "Han Shot First," and a gray jacket that came down to about his knees and matched his driving cap he'd worn the day before.

I saw Lucifer come down and I asked him, "What happened to my suit?"

All my life I'd tried to not take anything from my uncle because I didn't need anything and never have. I'd also tried to never take anything because I wasn't my shithead brother, who I am convinced is bankrolled by The Literal Devil.

"Nicholas," he chided, "your suit was in horrible shape. At least let me help you with this. For once."

"When did they get measurements to do this?" I asked him as I tugged lightly at the perfectly tailored suit.

"What do you mean?" he asked, bemused.

"I mean this is tailored."

He laughed. "Nicholas, as a half-fallen angel, there are advantages."

"What do you mean?" I figured if I'd had some kind of divine genetic advantage I'd be handsomer, taller, better with the ladies, packing in the pants, and better with grammar. I was none of those.

"Well, haven't you ever noticed every suit you've ever put on fit regardless of size?"

To be honest I hadn't thought about it. To a tall person the top shelf of a cabinet has no challenges but if your short, it might as well be the surface of Mars.

He chuckled. "You've not noticed, have you?"

"No, actually," I admitted. "So every suit fits me?" I was never going to get in the Avenger's with super powers like that. "Any cool powers I should know about?"

"Well, most of the time you're seen but not noticed. You got that from your mother. It's made you good at your chosen profession, but admittedly it's been hard on relationships, so it's not that your invisible, it's just that to most people, you're... forgettable."

I'm still not sure what the natural reaction was supposed to be in finding out that the reason you've been never been successful with the ladies is they simply don't notice you, but I always had a knack at tailing and surveillance. Double-edged sword? Double-edged Fiery Sword?

"Anything else?" I asked.

He thought a moment. "Eh, no, not really." He smoothed the suit over my shoulders. "What is your plan now?"

I shrugged. "Run, probably."

He nodded. "That's probably the wisest plan. That said," he smiled devilishly, "I'm not sure you can pull off *wise*."

Uncle Lew walked us to the Ped-Gate at the back of his property. He shook hands with Jammer who asked, extremely concerned, "I don't owe you my soul for the clothes and stuff, do I?"

Lucifer laughed. "No, I only buy the souls of aspiring Blues-Men at midnight at a crossroads in Mississippi." He shook Jammer's hand with his right and clapped his shoulder with his left. "Your soul is safe." He did pause for a moment and asked gravely, "How much do you really think your soul is worth, anyway?"

He didn't give Jammer time to answer before he turned and gave Gretchen a hug. He whispered something into her hair. I couldn't hear what it was, but it made her blush and hug him harder.

I stepped up, submachine gun under my coat, .45 under my suit jacket. I shook his hand and we pulled each other into a one-armed hug. I started to step out the gate but stopped and turned back.

"Why me?"

He smiled as if he had been waiting on that question. "There are two answers. What I'd tell you and what the Father would tell you."

"Let's start with you."

Lucifer looked me in the eyes and said, "Your mother stole the sword and hid it from Heaven and Hell because she knew the stakes. But she knew she would end one day, it was safer in the hands of a mortal. She had two sons."

"Why me?" I reiterated.

He smiled. "She asked my advice. I told her you." He shrugged. "I just had a good gut feeling."

I chewed on that for a second. "What would the Father say?"

"To what?" Lucifer looked confused.

"Why me?" I asked.

The Devil laughed. "He'd lean in, shrug, and whisper, '*Why Not?*'"

With that Lucifer turned and ambled back up the gravel path, hands stuffed in his pockets. "You've always reminded me of me, Nicholas," he called over his shoulder.

"Why's that?" I called out.

"Because we do things for the same reasons."

"And what's the reasons?" I asked, because to be honest I hardly ever knew my reasoning for things. I'm kind of an Occam's Razor dude.

"Because fuck you, that's why." He laughed and disappeared in the house. That answer did make sense.

Jammer led the way as we headed back through the woods to the car. There wasn't a lot of talk; any even. What was there to say?

We got to the car and pulled the gun duffle out of the trunk and put it in the back seat. I stood by the driver's door, Gretchen the passenger's door, and Jammer next to her.

"So what's the plan?" Jammer asked.

"They're looking for us back in town," I said as I looked between the two of them, "so seems to me hiding right under their noses might be tough, but it's the best play."

Jammer nodded in agreement. Gretchen didn't argue. Two things happened simultaneously: I heard the roar of motorcycle engines and a flash bang went off right behind Gretchen and Jammer.

The car shielded me from the flash bang and being out in the open helped dissipate the pressure, but it still knocked the two of them senseless. Gretchen went down and Jammer stayed up only by grabbing the car for support.

My ears were ringing, but I was up. I pulled the MP-10 from under the coat and got the butt-stock extended and to my shoulder. I turned to face the engine noise even as I scanned for who threw the flash bang. I dropped to my knee aiming down the sights as I saw the six bikes come over the rise.

"Jammer!" I roared. "Grab her and run!" Then the submachine gun roared for me. The first bike wavered as my three-round burst punched three holes in its rider's chest. Both bike and rider went down. I could see muzzle flashes coming from the other riders. I heard the impact of rounds hitting the car as I cooked off another three-round burst. I took out the headlight of one of the bikes as the other two rounds took out the rider. He and the bike wavered and slammed into the bike next to him, crashing both.

I was pretty sure I could hear Jammer moving but my ears were still ringing from the stun grenade. I knew there was nothing I could do right now on that side of the car and I had plenty to do here.

I heard rounds hitting closer. I rolled away from the car onto the road and laying prone, I aimed and fired a third three-round burst. The tire of the lead bike shredded, and the biker went down with his machine. I watched his helmetless head bounce off the concrete and I swear I could see it come up off the road already misshaped before it hit again and drug on the ground this time.

I got up to one knee getting aim on one of the last two bikes. They were close. No more than twenty-five yards and about to pass me. I squeezed the trigger while aiming at the closest, then spun around, tracing the other as he blew past. I never took my finger off the trigger. I emptied the magazine, but I killed the two assholes. Fair trade.

I came to my feet and dropped the 10mm magazine, pulling the spare I had in the coat ramming it into the well and dropped the bolt. I scanned for Gretchen and Jammer and saw Jammer only forty yards from the car and still clearly out of it. He had the HK P-30 in his hand. He was fighting two men, but not Heaven's Hotdogs. His new opponents were guys armored in plate-carriers, helmets, and tactical gear.

Jammer put two rounds into the first man's chest, but the ballistic plates soaked the rounds. Jammer was aware enough to drop his aim and pump two more rounds into the man's hip... *that* wasn't armored. The man screamed and went down as shattered bone rubbed shattered bone.

Both men had suppressed MP-5's slung over their backs but that wasn't the weapon in their hands. They were holding tasers. The man on the ground fired and buried the barbs in Jammer's thigh. The second man in Tac Gear fired and shot his taser barbs in Jammer's back.

Jammer's whole body went into convulsions. God love him though; he managed to squeeze off another 9mm round into the guy on the ground. It was probably bad luck that it hit the guy uselessly in the plate carrier again, but you gotta love a guy who keeps squeezing the trigger even when he's well and truly fucked.

I brought the submachine to my shoulder and fired. The man still standing had a plate carrier protecting his chest and a helmet protecting his head, but those pieces of personal protective gear didn't do anything when I shot him in his face. He went down like a sack of shit, dropping his taser.

The man on the ground looked to me in horror and dropped his taser. He was smart. He didn't try to get the submachine gun off his back, instead he went for his pistol on his hip. If he'd had a drop-leg and was angled differently, he might have gotten it clear, but his pistol was high on his hip and he was on his back nearly laying on it while keeping pressure off his wounded side.

I watched him struggle with it through my sights. I watched the fear in his eyes and then the realization of what was about to happen, then the tidal resurgence of fear. In that instant, I saw the gamut of his basic humanity and in that instant, I made sure his funeral would be closed casket.

I moved to Jammer and kept scanning. I saw Gretchen, gorgeous and stumbling, down the road toward the crossroads. She had her pistol limply in her hand with defiant futility.

I started running to her, passing Jammer on the road. He wasn't going anywhere for a moment. That's when the van pulled up. The door opened and I thought she was dead. The twelve-gauge roared, and Gretchen went down.

A burst of belt fed fire, an M60 from the sound of it, roared from the van as two Tac Geared men leapt out and grabbed Gretchen.

I dove into the ditch as the belt fed threw up dirt. I tried to get my head and gun up, but it was a storm of belt-fed hell.

I heard the peel of rubber as the van tore off down the road. I came up, gun at the ready. The van was gone, and Gretchen was gone with it. My soulmate was gone. But she wasn't dead. Somehow I knew I'd know if she was dead. They had to have shot her with a beanbag round or something fucked up like rock salt. Why else take her? She wasn't dead. She couldn't be dead.

I started walking back to Jammer. There was probably a better way to get the taser barbs from him than just yanking them but that's the quality medical care he got. I pulled the plate-carriers off the two dead men. One was intact, the other Jammer had put enough rounds into it to probably crack the front ballistic plate. I threw them in the car as Jammer started pulling himself up.

He was on his hands and knees and laughed. He looked up to me. "I didn't pee."

I nodded my approval. "We got to go."

"Gretchen?" he asked.

"She's not dead," I assured him "but those mutherfuckers are, they just don't know it yet."

XXIII: ...The Metric of Love

The corner of Canal and Merchant had been a warehouse in the 1920's. It had that look of a building where the designers and builders had given a damn about the ascetic that modern, prefab structures just don't. The front doors were large and oak, meaning they'd be easy to bar from the inside. The large bay window wasn't original, and neither were the bars over it. It was a three-story structure but there were only two floors, the first was just very high and open.

My brother had always been more likable and popular. He'd always had a plethora of friends. I get what Stalin meant when he said, "Quantity is a quality all its own." Or something like that. He had more friends, but I had better ones. His would bail him out of jail, mine would be in there with me. If his friends were in jail with him, they'd dime him out in a heartbeat. My friends would kill for me.

There were two Heaven's Hotdogs on the roof. Who knew what kind of guns they had stashed up there? There was another two by the front door. There were twenty or thirty more douchebag Christian Bikers inside. They were ready for trouble. They weren't ready for war.

They weren't ready for us.

The first guy to die was one of the Heaven's Hotdogs on the roof. The shot took him in the ear and sprayed his brain on his buddy standing next to him. Fired from a Draganov less than a hundred and fifty yards away Yuri, might as well have pushed the gun to the side of the man's head.

In the next moment the Toyota Camry with a piece of scrap pipe pushing the accelerator to the floor plowed through the row of bikes in the front and slammed through the wall and plate window. I know for a fact that the car itself killed or maimed at least three Heaven's Hotdogs. The explosion of the gas cans in the back seat tripped with a shotgun shell, turned blasting cap wired to a burner phone, killed another five to ten and blew every window out of the place.

Yuri's second shot dropped the second guard on the roof by hitting him in the center of the chest, giving the man enough time to look down at his wound in surprise before falling to bleed out.

Jammer and I crossed the road at a sprint. Not a mad sprint or an Olympic sprint, but at a fast, tactical run. The MP-10 dangled from my shoulder and bounced as I ran, the Franchi SPAS-12 to his. Butt-stocks of both were extended. The plate-carriers of the two dead men covered our chests and back. I had the double barrel sawed off Gretchen had been using in my right hand and an Uzi I'd taken off a mostly dead biker I'd left in the road in my left hand.

I emptied the magazine of the Uzi into one of the bikers outside guarding the front door that was pulling his worthless short to live carcass from the ground, stunned to his feet. I dropped the empty Uzi as easily as I'd dropped the Biker.

Yuri's third shot lanced through the neck of the second door guarding biker.

I grabbed the flash bang from the plate-carrier I was wearing with my left hand and hooked the ring around my right pinky without moving my hand from the sawed-off. I tugged the ring free and glanced to Jammer. He nodded, and we yelled in chorus, "Flash Out!" before tossing the flash bangs through the car-created entrance.

The flash bangs went off in quick succession and Jammer and I followed. Some people were burned, and most were disoriented. Plenty weren't dead yet. The first person I came across was a woman wearing the vest of the Heaven's Hotdogs trying to pull herself up off the floor. I gave her one-barrel of .00 buck to the back of her head.

I could feel the rage pulling at me. Guilt or innocence didn't matter; if they were here, they were complicit. That was all the justification I needed, Fiery Sword or not. The only justification Jammer needed was he had my back.

I saw a guy in his sixties probably retired from some boring job trying to pull himself out of a chair. His wispy hair was singed and smoking. I gave him the second barrel of the sawed-off right in his chest. I saw a woman at the remains of the same table, probably his wife. I beat her head in with the shotgun. I don't remember how many times I hit her but I remember her head wasn't shaped like a head anymore. I dropped the bloody, empty weapon with her hair dangling from the connection of metal and wood.

That was the metric of love fulfilled. Love isn't measured in happy days, pleasant walks, candlelight meals, hugs, kisses, time, caresses, movies, Netflix and Chills, ice cream, pleasant conversations and chocolate... love is measured in the pain you're willing to endure and the horror your willing to inflict. Love is measured by the line you're unwilling to cross. Love in its purest form can be a terrible thing.

I was there for Gretchen. I would be her terrible savior or her righteous avenger. I was there for Gretchen and I was not walking away empty-handed. I felt the rage tugging at me, but I buried it. I didn't need it — not for this.

I brought the MP-10 to my shoulder. Jammer was at work and fires were already starting to cook from where he was launching Dragon's-Breath rounds like they were firecrackers and it was the Fourth of July.

I heard another Draganov shot and assumed Yuri was working the windows on the upstairs floor. I emptied an entire magazine, putting individual rounds into injured and groggy men and women as I went to the stairs. I changed it and heard Jammer reloading the tube of the shotgun behind me as I started heading up the stairs.

"Jammer, door." It was all I said. Jammer slid a breaching round into the tube and pushed the barrel up under my arm and past my chest. The shotgun roared and the door blew open as the lock disintegrated. I ran and barreled my shoulder into it and button hooked along the wall. Jammer was behind me and followed the motion of the door slamming it to the wall with his body.

As I cleared the deep corner and turned to cover the room, Jammer pushed the barrel of the shotgun into the crack between the door and the wall and lit the man he had slammed behind it on fire with the Dragons-Breath.

I saw a man running through the door toward us with a ridiculously large revolver. Then I saw his head snap back and he slid across the floor pistol clattering. Thanks, Yuri.

"Flash Out." I tossed a flash bang through the door, waited for the boom and then followed it. There were three men stumbling around in the smoke of the flash bang. I shot the first at near point-blank range in the head. Jammer poured through the door and caught the second man in the gut with the Dragons-Breath.

The third man held down the trigger of his machine pistol and sprayed. I heard Jammer grunt but didn't look. I put three rounds into the man's chest so tight it looked like one large hole.

I glanced to Jammer and he had been hit in his left arm. He saw my look. "Through and through. We'll deal with it later. Keep going!"

Jammer hit the next door with the burning rounds. They weren't as good as breacher rounds but they got the job done. The next room was the last on the top level. There were four women, a large burly looking guy, and a smaller guy in Heaven's Hotdogs vest and a clerical collar.

The large burly guy charged at me with a baseball bat. I guess he assumed this was the moment when we duke it out hand to hand like gentlemen, or at least men with bats. Fight by the Marquis of

Queensbury rules and all. Gentlemen go to your corners. Listen to all commands. Come out fighting.

I shot him three times in the chest and once in the head for good measure.

Jammer came in behind me, saw that the situation was well in hand and tossed me the shotgun. He moved to a corner and started working on his arm.

I moved slowly across the room, each step slow and deliberate. I had the MP-10 in one hand and SPAS-12 in the other. Two women were on each side of the old man. Why the hell did he have four chicks around him if he was the head of a supposedly Christian organization? Crazy Christian Neo-Feminist? Was he an asshole cult leader? I knew what I'd put my money on.

"You the head Hotdog?" I asked coldly.

"By the power of Christ..." he began in an oddly nasal voice, it sounded like Gollum had a sinus infection.

"If you finish that fucking sentence," I said coldly, "I'm killing one of the women." I could feel the wrath tugging at me.

"By the power of Christ! I compel thee demon—"

I raised the MP-10 and shot the woman closest to him on the right. Her head snapped back, and she slumped against him. The others screamed and started to make a run for it, but it's amazing how much bullets landing inches from panicky feet fired from a submachine gun are better at halting forward momentum than stop signs.

I said coldly, slowly, "All I want is the girl the assholes in the van took."

"They weren't part of our club," The man gasped.

"But they were with you." My tone could have given someone frostbite.

"They were Teutonic Knights!" he screamed, "They were Teutonic Knights, they have her, they took her to him!"

"Who is him?" I felt a smile tugging at my lips. It wasn't a kind one.

"I can't say!" the man cried. He cried more when I shot the woman to his left. I didn't care. They didn't matter. The lives of shitty people couldn't matter. Just Gretchen — Gretchen was all that mattered.

"*You fuckin better say, Goddammit!*" I roared. He cringed at the blasphemy.

"Zadkiel. Zadkiel is with them!"

"Fucking where?" I pointed the shotgun one-handed at the woman on the left, the MP-10 at the woman on the right.

"They are at the church, Bell and 10th," the man cried. His body racked with sobs.

I watched them and asked quietly. "You okay back there, Jammer?"

"Yeah, I'm good." he called. "Nothing I can't fix later."

"Good. Sorry, brother."

"No big deal," he assured me.

I took a long moment. "Why don't you go tell Yuri thanks? Tell him I appreciate it."

He waited a moment and moved up to my side. "You trying to get me out of the room?"

"Yeah."

He stood for a second. "Okay, but don't go after Gretchen without me."

"Wouldn't dream of it." I smiled. It was predatory, like a wolf looking at a mutton dinner.

I heard Jammer leave.

"You know who I am?"

The man nodded.

"You know *what* I am?" I was quickly coming to grips with who and what I was. If these fucks wanted me to be the son of a demon and the nephew of the devil himself, so fucking be it.

I felt the rage pulling at me. I felt the Fiery Sword wanting to unsheathe itself and punish the unworthy who had failed the Throne and the Father's plan. I felt the Wrath of God wanting to set the fucking world on fire.

"Do you actually believe? Or is it just a game to you?" I asked quietly, keeping the guns trained.

"I Believe!" he cried.

"Saved by grace, you're on your way to Heaven if I do this. The Father's gonna welcome you with wide open arms and say *good job, bro*. You really believe that?"

He nodded, he wept, and he blew a snot bubble. "I do, the Lord is my Shepard I shall not want. He maketh me lie down in green pastures...."

He prayed the Lord's Prayer. It was too bad really. I would have felt better if he'd had doubt; if he'd wondered. I was pretty sure killing someone certain of his or her own salvation wouldn't be as good. Never had been with Hajj in the war. Maybe I just didn't get any satisfaction out of killing. Killing was like breathing; you just do it and don't think about it after.

"...but deliver us from evil!" he cried.

I don't know if God delivered them from evil. I do know he didn't deliver them from me.

Satisfaction or no, I killed them anyway.

Deserve had nothing to do with anything. They died because they were metaphorically standing between Gretchen and me. They died because their usefulness was spent like dollars at a strip club. They died because I wasn't going to look over my shoulder for the rest of my life for them. They died because someone took Gretchen.

I was going to get Gretchen back, or burn the fuckin world trying.

Love isn't measured in happy days, Hallmark Cards, breakfasts in bed, hand holding, fingers brushing across one's cheek, the effort to be there, the warmth between the big and the little spoon, date nights, jewelry, remembering dates of birthdays and anniversaries, supporting each other through trial and bouquets of flowers. Love is measured in atrocities. Love is measured in the terrible things we would do for the ones we love. Love is measured in the line we will not cross. Love in its purest form, can be a fucking terrible thing.

XXIV: Can't Beat Chuck Yeager and Tenzing Norgay

Jammer and I sat in the half-busted VW van we had acquired by the wrecked bar of the Heaven's Hotdogs. Our plate-carriers were on and a little worse for wear, but it wasn't like we could take them to the supply sergeant and get new ones. I hadn't look behind the bar for bottles of scotch or kegs of beer, I just assumed their clubhouse was some kind of bar. But with crazy Christian bikers, who knows? But I could have used a drink and my flask was as dead as Elvis.

We sat watching the church.

"There are a couple side entrances and a back one for deliveries for their shelter," Jammer said calmly. His arm bandaged up and a Fentanyl patch under his shirt. "Also the front one."

Lightening peeled and rain started falling hard, drumming on the roof and windshield.

"Maybe you should sit this one out Jammer," I suggested quietly.

"Fuck you." He sounded more vehement that I'd have thought.

"You've already been shot today," I offered.

"So?" he spat petulantly.

"This is my fight." That was true at least.

"You know what asshole," he growled, "if my girl were in there and I was about to do something stupid, you'd be right there with me, having my back, dick deep in stupid."

I couldn't help but smile.

"You're my best friend." Sometimes there are no not cliché ways of saying something so you just make due and sound like an asshole. "Fuck it. You're my brother."

"You fucking know it." He poked his bandage on his arm and smiled, apparently the fentanyl patch was working. He saw me watch him poke his arm and muttered an unconvincing, "Ouch."

"I do wish we had more help though," Jammer admitted slowly.

I sighed. "Yuri isn't built for CQB anymore."

"No," Jammer agreed. "Sending him home was the right call. I wish Switch was here."

I nodded in agreement. Switch was an engineer we knew from the 82nd Airborne. Not engineer as in, "I design stuff or work for NASA," but engineer in the military sense as in *I blow shit up for a living*. His last name was Kumar, but the problem with army buddies is a lot of times you never learn each other's first names. "Yeah, Switch could blow the fucking doors."

Jammer nodded in sad agreement.

I looked back and watched the front and side door. I saw the van that took Gretchen and I felt the violent tug, the tingling in my hand to go get her right now.

"Do we have a plan?" Jammer asked as he finished reloading the shotgun with a collection of Dragons-Breath rounds and 00 Buck.

"Not a great one," I admitted. No point in lying to your best friend, especially if you were probably gonna get yourself killed over a stripper you met two days ago, soul-mate or not.

"Goddammit," Jammer muttered. "Nick, who are your heroes?"

I thought about it for a moment. I narrowed it down to two actual people and not fictional characters. "Yeager and Hillary."

"That's right. Edmund Hillary and Chuck Fuckin Yeager." Jammer clapped.

"You getting to a point, Jammer?"

I could tell he was getting worked up. Jammer was bouncing his legs and clapped his hands together, obviously excited. "Hillary was the first dude to summit Everest, man. That's a big damned mountain. Yeager broke the fuckin sound barrier! People thought that was physically impossible and he made the sound barrier his bitch."

"Yeah, I know—"

"Dude!" He was hollering now, but when Jammer's enthusiasm got going you had to let that train run out of steam. "That Fiery Sword is your damned X-1. It's your, I dunno, boots or axe or whatever climbers use."

I nodded. "I'm kinda tracking. But there's a good chance there's an angel in there."

"Yeah, that dude. Edmund Hillary, first dude atop Everest. Chuck Yeager, dude who kicked the shit out of the sound barrier. Nick Fucking Decker, first dude to ever kick the shit out of an angel! We're gonna do this, bro! I'm your Tenzang Norgay... I'm your dude that sat in the plane and gave Yeager gum and a broom handle."

"Jack Ridley" I'll be honest Jammer's attempt at a Knute Rockne moment was actually getting my heart pumping.

"That's fucking right!" Jammer was bobbing his head front and back like a metronome. "Now who is in there." He pointed to the church.

"Gretchen."

"And who is she, bro?" Jammer slapped my knee.

"She's my fuckin soulmate."

"Yeah!" Jammer yelled. "And who the fuck are you?"

"I'm the guy that wants to have sex with her!" I yelled, no denying I was pumped up now. "Again!"

Jammer stopped and looked crestfallen. "Come on, dude. I was on a roll, don't fuck this up."

"Nick goddamned Decker?"

He smiled. "You are Nick *Fucking* Decker!" He then grabbed my shoulders and with all the sincerity ever mustered by a mortal man said, "And I am your father!"

I stopped and sat back. "Huh?"

"I'm your father," he repeated with less assurance.

"Jammer..." The confusion in my voice wasn't about what he said as opposed to the why. "I'm like two years older than you."

Again, he looked like someone had taken the last grape mini box of nerds from the bag and left only strawberry. "Sorry, I just, I don't know, kinda felt I was on a roll."

"No, it's cool. You were on a roll," I assured him.

Jammer smiled awkwardly. "Should we pray or something?"

"Is that gonna make you feel better, buddy?" I asked curiously.

"Kind of yeah," he admitted, embarrassed. "You can take the boy out of the catholic school, but you can never spank him with a ruler, I guess."

I chuckled. "Got any prayers in mind?"

"Boondock Saints prayer?" he offered.

"Eh, that's more climatic and not pre-battle."

"Yeah," he agreed reluctantly.

I felt everything. The insanity of the past few days and the new madhouse knowledge that had come with it crushed my brain. I felt the anger pulling at me. I didn't know if it was actually mine or if it belonged to the Sword. Did it even matter in that minute? The absurdity hit me like a baseball bat.

I did my job buzzed most of the time. I keep a flask in my pocket and use it more than I normally use my pistol or my camera. And let's be fair, that camera was usually what paid the bills.

I sat in a van with a submachine gun in my hands ready to go in and murder a bunch of people to get back my soulmate... how stupid did that sound? About to assault a church with a pistol, a submachine gun, a mystical sword that I could barely control, and my best friend who had stuck with me since...

I smiled and looked to Jammer's reluctant concerned face. "Jammer, what's best in life?"

Jammer's face lit up like a Christmas tree. "To crush your enemies, see them driven before you, and to hear the lamentations of the women." Jammer usually needed no prompt to quote *Conan the Barbarian* but today, he came through regardless.

We looked to each other and nodded solemnly and simultaneously started praying. "Crom, I have never prayed to you before. I have no tongue for it. No one, not even you will remember if we were good men or bad. Why we fought, or why died. All that matters, is that two stood against many. That's what's important. Valor pleases you Crom, so grant me one request. Grant me revenge! And if you do not listen... then to hell with you!"

We high-fived, then clutched each other's forearm. If you'd asked me to walk against an army with only one man, I'd pick Jammer; well unless Chuck Norris wasn't busy, anyway.

"Chuck Yeager," I told him with pride and piety.

He nodded again. He was getting back in his groove. "Chuck fucking Yeager, man!'

I didn't think. I was past thinking. Thinking had never been my strong suit anyway, planning even less so. General Patton said something along the lines of, *better a bad plan today executed violently than a perfect plan tomorrow*. I had one thought.

Fuck it.

I grabbed the submachine gun and pushed open the door of the van. I got out in the pouring rain and started striding to the front door of the church. No hesitation.

"Nick!" Jammer yelled. "What the hell are you doing?"

I held up the HK MP-10 in my right hand like a kid in the movie *Red Dawn* with an AK. "CHUCK FUCKIN' YEAGER!" I got to the front door of the church and kicked it as hard as I could, then I realized it was a pull door.

I grabbed it with my left hand and yanked it open. I crossed the threshold with the submachine gun to my shoulder. It was barely lit and the storm outside didn't give a lot of ambient light through the lovely stain glass windows.

The sanctuary was empty except for a large man. He was tall – not unnatural basketball player tall – but definitely outclassed five-foot eight me. In the dim light his ebony skin seemed unnaturally dark and his eyes unnaturally bright. In his left hand he held a violet cowboy hat. He wore a long violet flowing duster. He looked calm as he looked at me staring down my weapon's sights at him.

"You have your mother's eyes." His deep voice rumbled like a storm that ate a train and then farted.

"All I want is the girl." I thumbed the weapon from safe to auto. It felt good. "All I want is Gretchen."

"And all I want is the Fiery Sword." He seemed calm, in that cracked levy kind of calm.

I smirked. "One of us will be happy today."

He started walking toward me down the row of pews.

"I'll kill everyone in here," I growled.

"Like you murdered the Heaven's Hotdogs?" He didn't sound angry, bemused, annoyed, irked or any emotional adjective I could think of. He was as filled with caring as the iceberg that stuck it to the Titanic.

"Tempt me, motherfucker." I put my finger on the trigger and he kept coming.

"That's your Uncle's job." I couldn't tell if that was sarcastic or not. I was getting a bit past caring at that point.

I felt my teeth grinding together. "Did you kill my mother?"

He smiled sadly. "I remembered her before the fall. It pained me to end her." He slowly started stepping toward me. There had been genuine regret in his voice that time. But I was feeling less than sympathetic.

"Fuck it." I muttered those two words, which can give a grunt hope while simultaneously sustain him through dark times and opened fire, fully automatic. I turned on the Tac-Light and hit him in the face with it. But apparently spending eternity staring up the Father's kilt as he squatted on the Throne made you immune to bright lights because he never wavered or blinked. I emptied the entire magazine of thirty 10mm rounds into his chest and he just kept coming. He might as well have Bugs Bunny'd the gun by sticking his finger in the end of the barrel for all the effect the rounds had as they impacted. He grabbed the MP-10 and tore it from my hands, breaking the sling connection, and punched me square in the chest. Yet instead of a normal punch, I flew back five feet and hit the door. Needless to say, that fuckin hurt. I groaned as I pulled myself to my feet.

"I am Zadkiel, Bannermen of the Armies of the Throne. You, Nick Decker, are nothing." He charged at me. It wasn't running like if I had charged at him. It was one powerful step then a levitating flying deal. He came on fast too. It was at this moment I regretted not really planning this out like Jammer seemed to have wanted to.

I dove to the left and he flew past hard enough to tear the front doors off the church when he crashed into them. I ran and leapt on to the back of the pew and started running along their tops toward the front of the church, my Chuck's finding purchase on each pew back and hoping I just didn't eat it. Not because I didn't want Zadkiel catching me, but because I didn't want to look stupid.

I leapt from the first pew and landed feet shoulder width apart and knees bent. I knew it would hurt less to roll with it, so I did. I rolled and came back up to my feet. I felt the anger. I felt the wrath. He was between Gretchen and me.

The Fiery Sword leapt into my hand quicker than a fourteen-year old's wang into his hand the second he was home alone. I came up by the alter and raised my arm, pointing the burning blade down the aisle. I saw Zadkiel; he reached under his long duster and drew a long, thin blade that seemed to be made of pure white light.

"Is this the way you wish it, Decker?" he asked. "Give me the sword and I'll see that you and the girl, the stripper, are reunited in the Father's house."

"If one raven hair on her head has been hurt I'm going make you like Disco!" I could feel the fire.

"Disco?" he asked confused.

I sighed. "Dead, motherfucker. Disco is dead."

He cocked his head to the side in confusion. He seemed as confused about me as I was about his pimp outfit. For a moment, he seemed unsteady.

I felt a smirk touch my lips. Oddly, for the first time since trying to kick the door in did I feel any confidence in what I was doing. "You are gonna fuckin lose." The burning blade felt firm; mighty in my hand.

"Oh?" he said as he started down the aisle. "No man has ever defeated an archangel, though better than you have tried."

"I know something you don't." I pulled the blade back and put both hands on it. It grew longer in my grasp. I felt the rage. I felt the tugging in the back of my mind. And I saw, truly saw. I could tell from his grip that his first swing would come from the left. I didn't know that on my own, but the Fiery Sword knew that... so I knew it. My life had become a jacked up circular diagram.

"And that is?" His step faltered. Apparently, the unknown fucks with Archangels the way it fucks with normal people.

I smiled. "At your core, at your most freakin basic, you're just a fucking virgin with a low rent lightsaber, and me..." My smile must have melted into a smirk, "I'm an asshole armed with the Wrath of Fucking God. So give me Gretchen, or Daddy's gonna fuckin spank you."

Behind Zadkiel I saw Jammer slide through the broken doors with the shotgun and start heading downstairs. Jammer was going to find Gretchen. One way or the other, it was all on Jammer. I had a job. I had to distract the archangel. It sounded simpler than the reality would prove to be.

Our blades met in a flash of light and fire. Zadkiel had swung from the left and I turned it with the Fiery Sword. There was a look of surprise on Zadkiel's face when my blade didn't give way. I smirked and that seemed to annoy him. I felt the rage and gave myself to it. He struck again and I parried, then I would counter thrust and he'd parry or dodge. It was the world's most unsexy dance. Our blades clashed again and again in sparks of fire and light. Several pews were on fire from where the Fiery Sword had cleaved clear through them.

In the background I heard the gunfire. Jammer was mixing it up with someone, or from the sound of it, several someone's. I heard shotgun fire that was rapid enough to have been fired from some semi auto shotgun. But the gunfire kept singing, so I knew Jammer was still in the fight.

I was still in the fight. Uncle Lew said I'd be better with weaponry. Considering all I knew about sword fighting was what I'd seen in movies, I was holding my own rather well, until he threw the kick, anyway.

It caught me in the chest. I flew up and back and crashed through the stained-glass window. I hit the wall on the other side of the alley and fell. That had hurt. I should have died, but I didn't. I guess it was the Fiery Sword making me tougher.

"Drunkards and lovers, I guess," I heard Zadkiel rumble at the end of the alley.

I stood slowly and unstrapped the plate carrier and dropped it. The chest plate was in several pieces from that kick. I dropped it with a clatter into a puddle.

The world lit up as the lightening cracked across the sky. Water dripped down the walls and pooled onto the alley. My suit was soaked, and water streamed down my face; my usually unruly hair was matted to my head. I looked down the alley and saw him standing there in his long, gracefully flowing violet trench coat and cowboy hat.

"It's easy Nick... all you have to do is give me The Sword." His voice was a thick molasses-like bass. He sounded like the bastard child of Barry White and a Glacier.

I raised my 1911 and aimed the .45 ACP pistol, proper grip in the modern isosceles stance. Proper grip, proper sight picture, I thumbed the hammer back.

His voice rumbled through the downpour. "You know that's not going to work on me, at worst it's a bee sting, at best it's a nuisance."

I knew he was right. I let the pistol slide from my right hand to my left and fall to my side. I looked down at my right hand. I thought about Uncle Lew. I thought about Gretchen and wondered if she was even alive. I thought about my trashed car. I thought about my smashed bottle of Macallan 18. I thought about my wrecked office door. I thought about my dead goddamned mom. I felt angry. I felt mad. I felt pissed the fuck off.

I watched the pommel materialize in my palm and my fingers curled around it. I heard the hiss of water turning to steam as it landed on the growing blade. A blade made of fire.

He smiled. "Good. Give me The Sword, Nick, and all this ends. You can have your life back."

I looked at the Fiery Sword, then I looked to the archangel at the end of the alley dressed like a very expensive 70's pimp.

"You want the Fiery Sword, Zadkiel?" I gestured with the .45 in my left hand. "Then *Molan Labe,* you piece of shit."

Zadkiel smiled. "You know that is plural in the Ancient Greek."

I sighed. "Goddammit..."

"Watch the blasphemy, please." There was a crack in the glacier voice as if an iceberg was breaking off.

"Fuck you." I slowly shook my head and lifted the Fiery Sword. "You want it, you piece of shit come get take it from me Charlton Heston style."

Zadkiel took off his cowboy hat and ran his hand over smooth hairless head that was somehow still glowing even soaked in the storm. "I'm not familiar with Heston style."

I was about to get my ass kicked, probably killed, horribly. "Out of my cold dead hand, motherfucker."

Lightening flashed and we charged at each other. The Fiery Sword in my hand, the blade of light in his. I was done running. Our blades came together high and with my left hand, I shot Zadkiel in the knee. I saw him grimace. I jabbed the Fiery Sword at his chest but he parried it away, but not before I shot him in the knee again.

He brought his sword down in a mighty chop, which I barely sidestepped but managed to shoot him in the same knee a third time.

A rumbling roar escaped his throat as I feigned left but swung the sword right. He parried the blade down and I managed to rake it along his leg, slicing through his pant leg and angelic flesh. I also managed to shoot him in the knee again.

"Ahhh!" he yelled and swung. I ducked under it, but he did cut a dumpster in half with the swipe. As I was bent low I shot him in the knee for a fifth time.

At best it was a nuisance, at worse it was a bee sting. But a swarm of bees could kill a man just a sure as the distraction of a nuisance could in a fight. A sixth .45 ACP bullet hit his knee when I got my opening. He looked down. I didn't need the Fiery Sword to let me know this was the moment. I swung the Fiery Sword with every ounce of strength in my arm and felt the power of the rage in my breast flow into it and through it, and through me.

Zadkiel's head rolled onto the wet pavement of the alley. His body and head started to glow and then flashed, like a cube atop an old camera. Then, there was nothing but soaked pimp-clothes and a nine-inch in diameter gold ring spinning there on the puddled concrete.

I felt the rage burning in me. I slashed the nearby dumpster sheering it in half and leaving melted and curling ends. I stabbed into the brickwork of the church and walked a few paces, leaving a long, ragged gash in the masonry. I hacked twice into the alley's manhole cover sending it down in quarters. I roared like a madman. I was seeing red; red creeping into the edges of my vision making everything focused. I wanted to use the blade to light the church on fire. I wanted to use the blade to light everything on fire. I could feel it start to consume me. I could feel myself giving in. It felt like I was drowning, and it felt liberating all at the same time. I was free! Free to burn the world.

Then I heard the voice of an angel calling my name.

Epilogue?

I've not gotten to ask Lucifer about it, but I'm convinced Hell is a lot like Little Saigon Mega Awesome Disco Karaoke.

We sat eating finger foods in Room #3, while Jammer sang Bonnie Tyler's, *Total Eclipse of the Heart* with Joy with an E-Y providing the "Turn Around" and "Turn Around Bright Eyes."

Gretchen sat lying back against my side, her feet propped up on the couch laughing at the sincerity of Jammer and much to his annoyance. He had his arm in a sling. She'd ended up pulling twenty pieces of shot out of his arm and side where the plate cover hadn't, well… covered, that he'd taken getting her out. Jammer had cut his way through four flunkies and two actual Teutonic Knights to get to her.

For me, though, the real hero of the story was the heroine. I beat the archangel. Jammer might have saved the girl, but she saved me. The first time I used the Fiery Sword, I got knocked out when the car crashed. At Peaches, I felt the Wrath start to take me, but it was Gretchen who pulled me back. Then at the church, to beat Zadkiel in order to get Gretchen back, I was willing to give myself to it. Even after I felt the pull of the Wrath in my mind wanting to overtake me. At that moment, I had been about to unleash it all. Then Jammer and Gretchen emerged in the alley. She'd sent Jammer clear. He saved her from the Teutonic Knights, so in return she saved him from me. Gretchen hadn't flinched. She reached in and pulled me out of the burning hole in my own mind. Gretchen saved the world from me, and she saved me from me.

I don't know what the more noteworthy accomplishment was.

We'd gone back to Jammer's and Gretchen pulled the pellets of shot from his arm and got him bandaged up. Then she contacted Joy with an E-Y and got her to come back. That night, Joy nursed Jammer and probably other things I never want to know about. Gretchen and I crashed in the remains of my office, arm in arm, together.

The next day we got together at Little Saigon Mega Awesome Disco Karaoke.

If love is measured by the horrible things you'd do for someone, then I guess I love Jammer enough to go to "Asian Karaoke." Did that mean I love him more than Gretchen? All I did was kill a bunch of people and fight an archangel for her.

"You'd do better Bonnie Tyler than Jammer," I whispered into her hair.

Gretchen looked up to me and smiled. "I'm going to do Bonnie Tyler."

"But they took the good one."

She smiled. "No, they didn't."

"Oh?"

"My new Nick song. *Holding Out for a Hero*." She reached back and up to touch my face. That made me blush.

The door, which we had locked, opened without a sound. All eyes shot to the door and Lucifer stepped through. He politely shut it behind him. He waited until *Total Eclipse* was over and then heartedly applauded, then took a seat on the couch. Gretchen moved her feet to make room.

Lucifer wore a light linen suit. It looked a lot like the one Gary Oldman had worn in *The Professional* as Stansfield.

Lucifer looked up to Joy. "Joy, my dear, would you be a doll and give us a moment?"

She smiled. "I'm just going to go powder my nose."

She left and left me wondering did she mean fix makeup, take a leak, a dump, or do blow in the bathroom? All seemed viable options, including the combination of all four

The door closed, and Lucifer looked to us all but let his eyes rest on Gretchen. "I'm glad you're safe."

"Thank you," she said, smiling. Her smile could make me feel light enough that I knew if we could turn it into a weight-loss pill, we could make millions.

His eyes then turned to me. "Nick, I'm in the uncomfortable position of needing a favor."

My eyes narrowed. "What kind of favor would you need, Uncle Lew?"

"Please, just call me Lucifer, it's refreshing, what with us finally being on equal terms." He smiled, but there was embarrassment behind it, like needing a favor was shameful.

"What's up?" I asked quietly.

"Well, it's rather embarrassing," he confessed.

Jammer laughed. "We're good with embarrassing."

Lucifer smiled. "Well you see, I've lost my dog..."

I felt the corners of my lips turn up in a smirk. "The fuck?"

Hell for the Company Soundtrack

Nick:
Drivin n Cryin - "I'm Going Straight To Hell"
Theory of a Deadman - "I Hate My Life"
Flogging Molly - "The Worst Day Since Yesterday"
The Rolling Stones - "Streetfightin Man"
Chris Knight - "It Ain't Easy Being Me."
Lit - "Over My Head"

Gretchen:
David Bowie - "Modern Love"
Pat Benatar - "Hit Me With Your Best Shot"
Joan Jett - "Bad Reputation"
Sia - "Unstopable"
Liz Phair - "Extraordinary"
Meredith Brooks - "Bitch"

Jammer:
Eric Clapton - "Cocaine"
Bob Dylan - "Mr. Tambourine Man"
Framing Hanley - "Lollipop"
Smile Empty Soul - "Bottom of the Bottle"
Johnny Cash - "Sunday Mornin' Comin' Down"

Nick and Gretchen:
Bon Jovi - "Livin On A Prayer"
Halestorm - "Apocalyptic"
Johnny Cash - "I Walk The Line"
Theory of a Deadman - "Bad Girlfriend"
AC/DC - "Shook Me All Night Long"

Dedication

There are six groups/individuals that have to be thanked.

First and foremost: My wife Sharon, who is deceptively supportive of all my insane misadventures. Suspiciously supportive... I don't know your game pretty lady but I'm onto you...

Next I have to thank the Delta Writers Group, for simply showing up.

To the Tweeder, Bonds, Trent, Quintar, Marc, Kevin and Brad, and Sarah, who almost killed my Mom by asking if she were MY mom and not my Brothers, Kevin and Andrea, Mike and Kay, Timmy, Mike and Melanie, Phil and Teresa, and all those who were fans before there was a reason to be.

Fourth, thanks to Dr. Mark David Sheftall. As a mentor you really need to check your mentee screening process... some sketchy people have slipped through. Namely me.

Fifth, I will always be in debt to the men of B co 1/505 PIR 82nd Airborne, especially 3rd Platoon. I have never been better than when I was allowed to stand shoulder to shoulder with you boys in some less than polite places and hurt some bad people's feelings.

Lastly, to Brendan S. Hoffman, no man has ever had a better Brother.

So thanks.

About the Author

A veteran of the 82nd Airborne and a graduate of Auburn University. Dick Denny is a disappointment to his family, a fun guy to be around, and a handy guy to have about in a pinch.

Other Titles Available from Foundations, LLC

Rogue

By Laura Ranger – Steve Soderquist

Chris and Lexi Denton led what they considered a normal life.

Lexi worked as a dance instructor at a local studio, and Chris was a successful broker at a firm in downtown Miami, Florida.

When Chris gets entangled with a crime boss who utilizes his talent for numbers to cover up deadly secrets, the pair soon discover much more than just Carlos Mandini's dark secrets, they discover their own.

Chris and Lexi Denton are not who they believed.

As they run for their lives from Mandini and his organization, who they are and what they are capable of, begins to surface. Their pasts are remembered, memories the government thought they had wiped out; the very government that created them.

Now locked in a struggle for their right to even exist, they soon find themselves combating others like them—enhanced government projects created since birth to supplement and aid other military projects. In a run for their lives they discover what they're capable of, incredible feats of mental and physical strength and skill.

Those in charge neglected to factor in the most important lesson Chris and Lexi learned on their own...

Love supersedes science.

Culminating in an explosive ending that will leave the reader breathless, the two make it their mission to do what they know must be done—assure the Lz Project is not only destroyed, but can never be reactivated...

Even if it means they sacrifice themselves.

The Aryan Secret

By Simon French

CIA agent David Conway is awakened suddenly by his pager. His grandfather, retired General Robert Conway, needed to meet with him. Events quickly elevate at a frantic pace as David and his partner Brian Wheeler secretly look into the mysterious past of the charismatic and handsome German candidate, Christof Melzer, who is the top contender for the next Chancellor of Germany.

However, Robert Conway sees some alarming similarities to Melzer and the long dead dictator of the Third Reich, Adolph Hitler . Unknown to the agents, there is a secret organization called 'The Black Order' who will stop at nothing from keeping the men from potentially uncovering the truth. This high stake deadly mission will take agents Conway and Wheeler to three continents until discovering Melzer's secret—a secret that may start World War III and drag the world closer to Armageddon.

EVIN
By A.S. Crowder

Eva has never seen the Forest of Evin, but her fate and the fate of the Forest may be intertwined.

Sinister forces seek to pull the Forest apart, and Eva may be the only one who can save it. Eva must travel between worlds to keep the Forest together...

...but the Forest of Evin thrums with power and the force tearing it apart may not be the only danger.

Dark Prisoner – The Kruthos Key
By D. Thomas Jerlo

Suna Di'Viao, the last of the Divenean race, has hidden from the world, blaming herself for the demise of King Markes and Queen Saliste. It's a fate she believes she deserves, but when she's summoned on a quest by a mysterious stranger, her Divenean heritage won't allow her to refuse.

DECEPTION

By Laura Ranger

Izzy's had a lifetime of liars make up her past. All that changes with Caleb Matthews who's genuine and sincere. He teaches her not all is black or white. After 25 years of marriage she begins to suspect there's more to her husband then what she's known. No matter how she tries, she can't find anything amiss. Is her paranoia from being deceived in her past sabotaging her future or is there something more she's missing?

Made in the USA
Middletown, DE
19 July 2018